THE PIRATE'S PHYSICIAN

A thrilling companion novella to the Sea and Stone Chronicles

AMY MARONEY

Cover design by Dee Dee Book Covers.

Map by Tracey Porter.

Join Amy Maroney's community of readers and get a free book by signing up at www.amymaroney.com

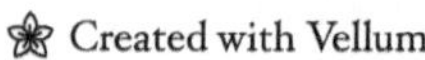 Created with Vellum

Sea and Stone Chronicles, 1400s
To FRANCE
VENICE
GENOA
CROATIA
FLORENCE
SIENA
ITALY
ALBANIA
ROME
NAPLES
SALERNO
SICILY
GREECE
Aegean Sea
ATHENS
BULGARIA
Black Sea
N
W
E
S
To ARMENIA
CONSTANTINOPLE
TURKEY
BODRUM CASTLE
ANTIPAROS
KOS
NISYROS
TILOS
KARPATHOS
*RHODES
CRETE
Mediterranean Sea
NICOSIA
*CYPRUS
SYRIA
BEIRUT
DAMASCUS
JERUSALEM
ALEXANDRIA
EGYPT
RHODES TOWN
ARCHANGELOS
LINDOS
ST. HILARION CASTLE
KYRENIA FORTRESS
ABBEY OF BELLAPAIS
NICOSIA
FAMAGUSTA
LIMASSOL
200 kilometers
200 Miles

CHAPTER 1

The Pirate's Physician

It's late afternoon, and the shadows grow long in Salerno's cobbled streets. Our rounds finally complete, Uncle Dante and I trudge uphill through the warm, still air toward home.

My stomach growls. I imagine the fresh squid with capers and onions fried in olive oil that our servant Rosetta will prepare for us tonight, then glance sidelong at my uncle's bowed head, his shuffling feet.

Not long ago, I struggled to keep up with him. Now he's the slow one.

I distract myself by silently reciting the Latin names for every bone in the human body. I've known the list by heart since I was twelve, and repeating the words is as calming as a prayer even now, a decade later.

"Is your mind full of bones?" Uncle Dante asks, throwing me a crooked smile. He knows my habits as well as I do.

I nod, lifting my skirts to avoid a rotten onion. "All I do is study for my examinations these days. I still wonder if it will be enough."

His smile deepens. "Concentrate on something you can't recite in your sleep. Like Trotula's remedy to ease a woman's monthly pains."

"Take five drams of saxifrage," I begin. "Add five more each of cloves, saffron, ginger, and . . ."

A shrill, childish voice calls out from behind us, "Professore! Wait!"

I turn to see a girl of about ten and a much younger boy careening through the street, dodging passersby. They accost us, panting, and the girl takes hold of my uncle's sleeve.

"Mamma is sick. Can you see her? Please?" The girl's troubled eyes vanquish my thoughts of home and supper.

"At once," Uncle Dante says in a soothing tone. "Lead us to her."

The boy lets out a whoop, turns on his heel, and races down the hill toward the harbor. His sister trots after him, imploring him to wait, but he ignores her. Soon, the two small figures begin to fade in the haze.

"Walk!" I shout in my most commanding voice. "What will your mother do if we lose sight of you?"

The girl seizes her brother by the arm and pulls him to her side. Hand in hand, they lead us into a cramped warren of streets inhabited by Salerno's poorest citizens.

We enter an alleyway that smells of piss and sun-rotted fish, then follow the children through the doorway of a small cottage. The girl gestures at a figure slumped on a pallet in a dim corner.

We approach the bedside. Uncle Dante stoops over the woman, lays a hand on her forehead.

She opens her eyes, and a slight smile of recognition

brightens her face when she sees him. Then her eyelids flutter shut again.

"She's hot," he says. "Not burning up, though." He throws me a questioning look.

"We need willow bark tea." I turn to the girl. "Fetch me a bowl of hot water. Take care not to burn yourself."

"Where do you hurt, signora?" Uncle Dante asks the woman.

"Everywhere," she rasps. "Especially my throat. It's aflame, I tell you."

The girl returns from the hearth with the hot water. I prepare the tea, adding plenty of honey from a small pot I keep in my satchel, and the woman drinks deeply from the bowl.

"Where is your father?" I ask the girl, low.

"At sea. He's a fisherman."

"Do you have something to eat tonight?" I ask.

"Yes. Dried whitefish, onions, and barley. Mamma usually makes the stew, but I know how to do it." She straightens her shoulders with a trace of pride.

I give her an encouraging smile. "Start supper then, *cara*."

The girl smiles back, pleased by the term of endearment, and gets to work.

Uncle Dante lifts the bedcovers and examines the ill woman's arms and legs, then gently presses on her abdomen, palpating her organs. He looks at me expectantly, and I conduct the same examination. There is a faint dark shadow along the woman's right cheekbone, and four barely visible fingertip-sized bruises on her left arm.

My chest tightens with a familiar tension. Too many women we treat suffer from more than illness and disease. They live under the constant threat of violence in their own homes.

"No skin rash," I report, careful to keep my voice even.

"No swellings, no sign of plague. Organs are healthy. Her color is not bad either, considering the fever."

Uncle Dante's vision isn't what it used to be. Did he see her bruises in the guttering candlelight? I hesitate to point them out, for he's been complaining of new aches and pains, worried that he's becoming an old man.

Bending down to the woman, I whisper, "Does he beat you often, your husband?"

"Not when he's fishing," she replies. "And not when his belly is full. I'm luckier than some."

"There's a convent where you can seek refuge if you need—"

"I know," she says flatly, her gaze sliding away from mine.

Outside, church bells toll the hour and dusk gathers. While the girl makes supper, I gently wash the young boy's hands and face with a length of clean linen.

"Principe," I croon to him. *"Tesoruccio."*

He throws his head back and laughs. "I'm not a prince! I'm not your little treasure!"

He's about the age I was when Uncle Dante took me into his care. Mamma was Uncle Dante's youngest sister. Not long after being widowed, she was struck down by a terrible fever. In my earliest memory, I sit by the hearth in Uncle Dante's kitchen, humming along to the rise and fall of Rosetta's voice as she hands me bits of dough to play with while she cooks.

The bubbling fish stew sends a savory aroma our way, and the ill woman casts a gaze at the hearth.

"I should eat a bit," she says.

The girl brings a bowl of stew and a spoon, and I help the woman sit up.

"My pain is better," she announces after a few bites. "Praise the saints. It's that tea, isn't it?"

"We'll leave some with you," Uncle Dante says.

I place the nearly empty bag of willow bark powder on

the bed next to her. Tomorrow, if fortune favors us at the harbor, we'll replenish our supply.

"I can't pay for that." The woman's voice is regretful. "As much as I want it."

My uncle shrugs. "You don't have to pay. It's my gift to you, signora."

A glimmer in her eyes betrays her gratitude. "God save you, signor. You're a good man, always have been."

He puts a hand over his heart. "Rest tonight, take more tea in the morning, and perhaps by evening you'll be making supper again."

As we walk home through the darkening lanes, torches affixed to the walls cast dancing shadows on the cobblestones. Uncle Dante strolls along, lost in thought, and I fight the urge to speed my step.

Three scruffy-looking men approach from the other direction, engaged in a loud, drunken conversation. I slip a hand in the crook of Uncle Dante's arm. My other hand moves to the dagger strapped on my belt. I've only used it once, and I pray I'll never have to wield it again. I watch the threesome warily, tensing my muscles. But when they see us, they draw back to let us pass.

"Professore," one of them says to my uncle, bowing a little. "Go with God."

Uncle Dante nods at them amiably. He's known in these rough lanes as a man of compassion and generosity, and the goodwill people feel for him keeps me safe, too. For a moment, I wonder how I'll cope when he's no longer walking alongside me. My throat thickens with emotion, and I bury the thought.

"What is your conclusion about the fisherman's wife?" he asks me.

"She has the same illness as most of the others we've seen today. Fever, sore throat, and pain that responds well to willow bark. A nuisance more than a danger, as long as she keeps eating and drinking." I take in a breath. "And her husband beats her. But not often, and not as violently as some men."

"Well done." He glances at me. "You're ready for your examinations."

Nervous anticipation flutters in my stomach. "Truly?"

"More than any other student at the Schola Medica today. I should know. I've taught them all, and not one is your equal. No one has exhibited such a brilliant mind for medicine since Trotula de Ruggiero."

I glow under the praise. Trotula de Ruggiero was one of the school's most esteemed and influential graduates, and her skill at diagnosing and treating women's ailments has never been matched.

Still, a sliver of uncertainty pricks at me.

I was admitted to Salerno's centuries-old medical school thanks to my uncle's influence. Unlike in Trotula's time, few women remain in the ranks of students or faculty these days. With Uncle Dante's help, I've managed to thrive in this mostly male world, driven by one constant wish—to be a physician specializing in the care of women.

Now, only weeks away from my dream becoming reality, it seems more distant than ever.

"There's so much to remember," I admit quietly. "It feels impossible at times to memorize it all."

He kisses my cheek. "Trotula's book is always there for you, *cara* Giuliana. Study it if you need reassurance."

I smile. Somehow we always return to the book.

CHAPTER 2

I SHADE my brow with a hand and study the harbor. Gulls circle and shriek overhead as fishermen maneuver small boats around merchant galleys anchored in the shifting waters. A basket of anchovies aboard one of the boats catches my eye, glittering like silver in the bright sun.

Uncle Dante and I amble along the dock, taking in the lively atmosphere. Sailors, fishermen, and housewives with servants in tow exchange good-natured chatter and greetings as they look over the goods being unloaded all around us.

"We need willow bark and plenty of it," I remind my uncle. "We're low on butcher's broom, poppy, and long pepper, too."

Instead of responding, he stops, distracted by the sight of a ship across the harbor. Its white banners, decorated with simple red crosses, flutter in the wind.

"I know that ship," he says slowly. "It belongs to a Florentine."

"A friend?" I ask.

A disconcerted look takes hold of his face. "Not exactly."

Before I can question him further, he waves a hand in the

air, gesturing at a sleek three-masted galley nearby. Its banners are emblazoned with curious interlocking black designs.

"Look at that handsome Basque vessel," he says. "Finely crafted, graceful in the water . . ."

Uncle Dante trails off as the Basque sailors lower a small boat overboard. Next, a rope ladder appears over the side of the galley, and several men clamber nimbly down into the little boat's hull. Two pairs of oars are soon dipping into the waves, propelling the boat in our direction.

The men emerge on the dock nearby. As they near us, I notice their linen shirts are decorated with intricate patterns of black thread that mimic the designs on the ship's banners.

The man in the lead is tall and lean, with a well-trimmed beard that does not quite cover curving scars on both cheeks. When he notices us, his eyes flash in surprise, and for a moment his fierce sun-browned face relaxes into an open smile.

"Professore!" he cries. "This can't be. It's the work of a goddess, I tell you." He throws back his head and addresses the heavens. "Mari, your gifts come without warning. Bless you."

Uncle Dante shakes his head in astonishment. "I thought I'd never see you again! Let me examine my handiwork, Captain Eneko," he says. "Approach."

Like an obedient child, the man stoops and allows my uncle to trace the lines of his scars with gentle fingers. The angles of the captain's face are sharp-edged, as if hewn from stone, and his face in profile is stark. The contrast between his flinty demeanor and his deference to my uncle intrigues me, and I stare at him with unabashed curiosity.

"You've healed beautifully," Uncle Dante marvels. "How many years ago was it?"

"I lost count," the man admits. "Haven't returned to Salerno since then; that's all I can say for certain."

"What happened?" I ask, looking from my uncle to the Basque captain in confusion. "What are you talking about?"

"You were home with me," Uncle Dante says. "A friend of mine brought a half-dozen men to the door, covered in blood. They'd been in a brawl. My friend swore they were respectable and would pay me in gold for my assistance."

"A group of Catalans at a tavern near the harbor called us pirates. One insult led to another, as they do. We came to blows," the captain explains, turning to me. "Signorina, I don't believe I've had the pleasure of an introduction."

"My niece, Giuliana," Uncle Dante puts in. "You may have seen the men cross our threshold that day, *cara*, but I had Rosetta keep you busy in the kitchen."

"It was the year I began my studies at the medical school." I can't help the note of accusation that creeps into my voice as the memories flood back. "You wouldn't let me help. And you performed cauterizations! I needed practice with those. I still do."

"You were too young," he chides me. "You weren't ready."

"I don't blame him for hiding you away," the captain says to me. "We looked grisly, and half the city believed we were pirates, thanks to those Catalans."

"But you're not pirates?" I challenge him.

"We Basques are fishermen, and we travel west in pursuit of whales and cod," he says with deliberation. "From time to time, a Basque will go his own way, though, sailing east to seek his fortune in gold."

The other Basques seem to be suppressing laughter. Is their captain mocking me? I look away from him, annoyed.

"Opening my door to you was the best decision I made that year," Uncle Dante says. "Most of my patients pay me in eggs and grain, not coin. I was grateful you paid me in gold—no matter what the Catalans called you."

"We're off to find a sea captain returned from Greece who's promised me precious cargo," the captain says, bowing to us. "In truth, I'd no desire to visit Salerno again, but now that I've seen you, Professore, I trust all will be well. I'll stop to pay you a call before we leave here, if I may."

Uncle Dante nods. "You're welcome anytime, Captain Eneko."

The captain seeks my gaze again, his mouth quirking in a half-smile that strikes me as cheeky. I blink and he's wheeling away, followed by his men. His stride is long and confident, his lean form outlined against the blue sky. Even if I didn't know he was their leader, I would assume they took their orders from him. There's something about the way he moves, with a loose-hipped power and grace that mesmerizes me.

I take Uncle Dante's arm, shaking off my reverie. "Let's visit the spice traders. There's a pack of housewives ahead of us—they'll take all the ginger root and cloves if we're not careful."

But he does not respond.

I glance at him, and my breath hitches in my throat. He sways, his face registering faint surprise, and his skin looks unnaturally pale.

"Uncle Dante! What's wrong?"

He sinks to his knees. I throw my arms around him and use all my strength to arrest his fall.

"Are you hurt?" I cry. "What's happened?"

"My blood . . ." he gasps, clutching at his heart. "It's not flowing as it should." He flaps his left hand into my field of vision. "Take my ring, by God!"

I work the gold signet ring from his finger, my breath wild, and slip it into my purse.

"Forgive me. I never intended . . ." His words stutter, his

face contorting with pain, then he grips my arm, his fingers digging like talons into my flesh. "After your exams, get to Genoa. To your aunt. She'll help you."

He falls silent, his head lolling against me.

"Shhh," I say. "Rest. Don't worry about anything but your breath."

He struggles, fighting for air. "The book! It must stay with you always."

The anguish in his eyes pierces me like the point of a blade.

I look desperately around. The departing Basques are fifty paces away.

"Help us, Captain! Please!"

The wind snatches my words and tosses them aloft. Fighting tears, I gulp air, trying to calm myself. When I shout again, my voice is strong and clear.

"Help us! For the love of God, help us!"

The Basques turn at the sound. I press my fingers against Uncle Dante's throat and am reassured by the faint rhythm of his pulse. The captain is at my side in the next instant.

"What's happened to him, signorina?"

"It's his heart, I think. We still have a chance to save him. Please!"

Signaling to a companion, the captain slips his arms around my uncle. The two men lift Uncle Dante as easily as if he were a sack of feathers and stride along the dock toward the city gates. I run-walk ahead, leading the way.

A friend of my uncle's, also a physician and a professor at the medical school, lives a stone's throw from the gate. We'll stop at his home first.

But we've not gone thirty paces when I hear a voice behind me. "Hurrying will not help, signorina. It's too late."

I turn.

The Basque captain's face holds a look of profound

sorrow. He and his companion cradle my uncle between them as tenderly as they would a loved one. A surge of grief floods me.

Uncle Dante is limp, his skin the color of ash. His eyes stare straight up at the sky, glassy and vacant. I lay my head on his chest, then take one of his hands and raise it to my lips.

"His heart has stopped," I murmur, my shoulders sagging. "His breath has failed."

Hot tears push at my eyes and cascade down my cheeks.

My beloved uncle is dead.

CHAPTER 3

IT'S A STILL, colorless day when I call upon Uncle Dante's lawyer with Rosetta in tow. We're admitted into his home by a dour old manservant and told to wait outside his office door. Apparently, this man possesses the only copy of my uncle's will. In a few moments, I'll learn what Uncle Dante has chosen to do with his home and belongings. What shall I do if the house and all our possessions are left to someone else? The worry digs a furrow in my mind.

Uncle Dante has never spoken of his will, nor given me a reason to doubt I'll be his beneficiary. Aunt Amalia and I are his only living relatives and the logical recipients of his estate. Still, the world turned upside down when he died, and a strong feeling of foreboding has settled in my bones.

I've had no appetite since my uncle's death. My nights have been restless, punctuated by nightmares. From the priest's first visit to the plans for the funeral and now this meeting with Uncle Dante's lawyer, I have moved through the world like a wraith, barely aware of my own living, breathing body, trapped in rumination about my uncle's death and my suddenly uncertain future.

Next to me, Rosetta sighs and squeezes my arm. I look down at her hand. It's mottled with an angry red rash. I dig in my purse for a small pot of ointment, uncork it, and dab a generous amount on her skin.

She flinches at my ministrations. "We've been waiting an age. There's nothing but silence on the other side of that door. Where is the man?"

"Rosetta, calm yourself." I try to keep the annoyance out of my voice. Rosetta's been in my uncle's household since I arrived there as a tiny girl, and I think of her as a nurse as much as a cook and a housekeeper. When she's worried, a river of words pours from her mouth.

The door opens, and the lawyer's long black tunic whispers over the tile floor as he waves me into the chamber. Rosetta makes to follow, but he shakes his head at her, and she huffs her displeasure.

"My condolences, Signorina Rinaldi." He closes the door and offers me a stool, then sinks down in the chair behind his desk. "Your uncle's death must be a shock. He was so helpful to so many. Salerno shall not be the same without him."

I nod, not trusting myself to speak. Sorrow threatens to choke me as I imagine Uncle Dante's body atop the supper table in our home, washed and dressed in his finest silk tunic and hose. Though Rosetta is allergic to lavender oil, she insisted on helping me cleanse his body with lavender water. Thus the rash on her hands.

The lawyer unfurls the will and holds it up to the light from the street-facing window.

"It's in Latin," he says. "Do you wish me to translate?"

I shake my head. "My uncle taught me Latin. You may read it as written."

"Very well." He clears his throat and begins reading. "*Ego Dante Rinaldi, compos mentis* . . . I, Dante Rinaldi, being of sound mind, establish and wish my executors to be my niece,

Giuliana, and my sister, Amalia . . .'" The Latin words wash over me with the rhythmic monotony of a Sunday mass, and I listen carefully to make sure I don't miss a detail. "Here follows the complete list of furnishings, plates, rugs, linens, and so forth. All destined to you, except for a family ring bequeathed to his sister and a bed and linens to his servant, Rosetta."

He pauses and glances at me.

"I am in possession of the ring," I tell him, "and I plan to deliver it personally to my aunt."

No need to tell him of Uncle Dante's dying words. *Get to Genoa.* I have much to do in Salerno before I can travel there —most importantly, finishing my studies. For now, a letter informing Aunt Amalia of his death shall have to suffice.

"And next, the house." His eyebrows rise in surprise as he reads, and his superior manner shifts into something more supplicating. "The home is to be left to you as well, signorina."

My clenched fists unfurl. The thread of worry spooled tight around my chest loosens at his words, and I take a deep breath for the first time in days.

What would I have done if the house and the possessions had not been left to me? But there's no one besides Aunt Amalia who is close to Uncle Dante's heart. Aunt Amalia is living a prosperous life in Genoa, and has no need of a home in Salerno. I'm certain Uncle Dante's youngest sister—my mother—would have inherited the house if she'd lived. But since her death, I'm all he has of her.

The truth is I have nothing of my own. Soon, when I pass my exams and start my own medical practice, I shall earn enough money to support myself. But not quite yet.

I close my eyes a moment, reeling off a prayer of gratitude in silence.

"There is a bit more correspondence to consider." The

lawyer reaches into a drawer and withdraws a letter written on fine linen paper, its red wax seal broken. "Your uncle brought me this some months ago, asked me to safeguard it for him."

I study the design imprinted on the face of the wax. Aunt Amalia is married to a Genoese wool merchant whose seal bears the head of a ram. This one depicts a full-body image of a sheep.

"It must be from my aunt," I say slowly. "Though the seal is different than I remember."

The lawyer spreads open the paper and smooths it with his hands. "This letter is not from your aunt. Did you know your uncle was indebted to a wool merchant of Florence?"

"No."

"It seems your uncle considered this man his personal banker. There's a list here of transactions over the past several years—he borrowed a great deal of money from the fellow. And paid it back in small installments. With quite modest interest." He scratches his head and adjusts his black velvet cap. "A banker or a moneylender would have charged him far more."

I absorb his words with a growing sense of bafflement. I know nothing about loans, interest rates, and bankers.

"My uncle had many friends," I say. "This man must be one of them."

"I'm afraid this is a complication your uncle did not foresee." He turns over the letter in his hands. "His death has changed everything. The merchant is in Salerno now, and his notary contacted me this morning. He wants his loan repaid in full."

I stare at him with trepidation. "How much money is it?"

"Two hundred gold florins still remain to be paid."

"But how can that be?" I splutter. "What did he need so much money for?"

The lawyer shrugs. "There is some explanation, of that you can be sure. Perhaps, with a bit of inquiry, you'll discover the reason. But your more pressing concern is this loan repayment. After all, you are now responsible for it."

My brain churns with questions, and I sift through them frantically, trying to think in terms of numbers rather than words.

"How many florins is my inheritance worth?" I finally manage.

The lawyer studies the will, his lips moving as he makes mental calculations.

"I would say about one hundred thirty florins. The house, furnishings, and other sundries."

I swallow. Even if I were to give my entire inheritance to this wool merchant, I would still owe him seventy florins! An image of the contents of my purse floats into my mind. It's all silver—a few handfuls of change that together add up to the value of a single golden florin. The impossibility of my dilemma forces all the air from my lungs. I struggle to take a breath, and my face grows hot. The lawyer pours me a cup of wine. I raise it with trembling hands to my lips.

Why did I never ask Uncle Dante about his problems, his interests, his dreams? All we spoke of was me and my plans. My uncle preferred not to talk about himself, even when questioned. It was simply his way. He looked outward, always nurturing others, ignoring his own needs.

I should have cared more about his future instead of prattling on about my own.

I put down my cup, trying to make sense of my uncle's actions. He never spoke to me of money troubles. He worked as a respected professor at the medical school in Salerno for decades. Like all physicians in Salerno, he treated the poor for no charge. But better-off patients paid him with coin for his efforts.

How on earth could he have driven himself into such great debt?

I look the lawyer in the eyes. "I'll find out what happened. I vow it. Perhaps when the period of mourning is over, I can meet with the wool merchant and ask for patience. Once I am a practicing physician, I'll earn a fine salary and pay back the loan myself."

The lawyer frowns. "I'm afraid he may knock at your door sooner than that. In his letter, the merchant asked for repayment of his loan as soon as your uncle's will has been read."

"What?" I say in alarm. "Does that mean—"

"Propriety dictates that he refrain from pursuing the matter until after the funeral," the lawyer cuts in. "But do not be surprised if you hear from him the very next day."

CHAPTER 4

At the funeral, I smooth my black skirts for the tenth time, studying the other mourners as they file into the church. There are a few richly dressed people in the crowd, including a couple I recognize as a nobleman's youngest son and his wife, patrons of Salerno's medical school. Which one of the others is the wool merchant?

The funeral expenses were all accounted for in my uncle's will. The small sum of florins remaining will barely cover daily expenses, school fees, and other essentials—let alone pay back the enormous loan to the wool merchant.

As the priest concludes his funerary mass, I inhale the stale, incense-scented air, determined not to cry. A woman seated nearby catches my eye and gives me a solemn nod. She's a butcher's wife who recovered from a terrible bout of fever last winter, thanks to Uncle Dante's ministrations. I return the nod, every muscle in my body tight.

Afterward, mourners approach me to offer their sympathies. Many are professors themselves, men I came to know during my years of medical school. Some are former patients like the butcher's wife, people who benefitted from Uncle Dante's gentle and wise care. A leatherworker's wife crushes me against her ample bosom with alarming force, her eyes leaking tears.

"You were everything to him," she says. "He loved you as his own daughter. What a grievous blow to lose him, you poor lamb. I shall bring you a pot of stew with beef and new peas. I'm sure you have not eaten a bite since he passed on, *cara*."

When I extricate myself and the woman moves on to greet the priest, two men appear at my side. One is a notary, a slight man with protruding eyes who often attends mass at the church. His companion is stockier and of middling height, his thinning hair covered by a green velvet cap, and he wears a matching short cape lined with fur.

"Signorina." The notary bows. "Please accept my condolences. Signor Rinaldi's death is a blow to us all."

"Let me express my deepest sympathies as well," his companion puts in before I can reply. "Signor Rinaldi was a man of good character indeed."

"Thank you." I regard the second man uncertainly. "Did you know my uncle, signor?"

"I did. I'm Antonio Lucchesi, wool merchant of Florence." His gaze runs the length of my body, then settles on my face. "You're quite lovely, signorina. I must admit I was not expecting that."

My stomach contracts. His speculative look is unnerving, and I fight the urge to cross my arms over my chest. The only thing I can think of to say is, "And you're a moneylender, too?"

The blunt words hang in the space between us. The feeling of disbelief I've been carrying around since my meeting with the lawyer has somehow seeped into my tone. He presses his plum-colored lips together, eyes narrowed.

"Not in any formal sense."

"How was my uncle acquainted with you, Signor Lucchesi?" I try to soften my voice.

"We met under regretful circumstances." The wool merchant smooths his cap with a hand, tugging it forward over his heavy brow. "I was quite ill, in Salerno for a visit to cousins who sell my wool at the market here. It was my bad fortune to sail into this city's harbor, for if I'd stayed away, I never would have fallen ill."

"Was it the plague?"

He crosses himself. "No, praise all the saints. It was some horrid fever. My neck grew thick as a tree trunk, and I could barely swallow or breathe. A concoction your uncle brewed kept me alive through the worst of it, and then I recovered over a period of weeks."

"That was when he started borrowing money from you?"

"I was happy to accommodate him, for he saved my health." He lets out a sigh. "But that was nearly ten years ago, and the wool trade in Florence is suffering now. I've learned generous gestures can be difficult to sustain when new challenges arise."

In my mind's eye, I see a ship with white-and-red banners, a vessel owned by a Florentine—a man my uncle hesitated to describe as a friend.

Now I understand the connection. Signor Lucchesi owes Uncle Dante his life.

"Did my uncle ever tell you what he needed money for? He had a salary from the Schola Medica, after all, and a medical practice."

"No." The man shakes his head with such force that his cap nearly flies off. "That was his business." He smells of bacon grease and amber oil, a combination that makes me want to hold my breath. "I mourn his death as much as anyone else, signorina, but I can no longer sustain the burden of his debt."

I stand taller. "Surely, this can wait until the period of mourning ends, Signor Lucchesi?"

"I will leave Salerno soon. I need to have this matter resolved before then."

"But you must understand my uncle did not have such a huge sum of florins at his disposal. I cannot pay his debt, not all at once. I have a proposition for you, signor." I force myself to hold the merchant's gaze. "I'll soon complete my studies at the medical school. Once I've established my practice, I will pay you back the money, with more interest than my uncle paid you, over a period of time."

He regards me with a long, unblinking stare. I feel like an object on display in a trader's market stall.

"You are not in a position to offer me a proposition, signorina," he says coldly. "It is I who will decide the terms of repayment."

The notary tents his fingertips against his chest and clears his throat. "Signor, it may interest you to know that Dante Rinaldi has a sister in Genoa, married to a wool merchant there, a man of quite high standing in the Genoese wool guild."

I am mystified by the comment. What does Aunt Amalia's husband have to do with this? But clearly Signor Lucchesi finds the notary's words intriguing, for the frown smooths from his brow.

"I see. Are you close to your aunt, signorina?"

I look from one man to the other, even more baffled. "Yes."

The corners of his mouth lift in a slight smile. "It must be a comfort to have the love of your aunt during this sad time."

"I have not yet sent word to her of my uncle's death. A message will go out on the next ship to Genoa."

He makes a humming sound in the back of his throat. "I believe we can come to an arrangement that benefits us both, signorina." His stance has relaxed, as has his tone. "Your lawyer will receive a letter from me tomorrow to that effect. Good day."

CHAPTER 5

SIGNOR LUCCHESI and his notary are already seated inside the lawyer's office when I arrive for our hastily arranged meeting a few days later. Once again, Rosetta is left to fume outside the door while I drag leaden feet into the chamber, acutely aware that I'm alone with three men, only one of whom is my ally. And even that is questionable. I can only hope the lawyer's loyalty to Uncle Dante extends to me as well.

A notarial register is open on the paper-strewn desk. A freshly inked page of words swims upside down before me. The lawyer begins to read the Latin text aloud while the other men look on with satisfaction.

To my absolute horror, I realize this is a marriage contract. My skin burns with a gathering tide of anger as I absorb the words.

The merchant has discarded my own idea—finishing school, beginning a practice, and paying him back in install-ments with my earnings. He's claimed there is only one acceptable solution: marriage to him.

The words spool out while I stand frozen, my future

crumbling before me. The marriage will take place within a week. Once the ceremony is completed, all of Uncle Dante's property will belong to Signor Lucchesi. Though that will not cover the extent of the debt, he will forgive the rest of the loan because of his generosity and his gratitude to my uncle.

The contract concludes by stipulating that Signor Lucchesi and I will visit Genoa annually so that I might spend time with my beloved aunt. I swallow, my throat dry as dust, and wonder if I misheard the lawyer. That unexpected measure of kindness softens the blow of the document somewhat, gives me a reason to hope that Signor Lucchesi might treat me well.

"This is quite generous," Uncle Dante's lawyer says when he finishes reading aloud. "You're a fortunate young woman. Much more fortunate than most. Signor Lucchesi is a wealthy, respected man. You'll run a fine household and bear him many sons."

Signor Lucchesi runs a critical gaze up and down my body. "No reason to suspect otherwise, is there?"

I want to slap him, and my resolve strengthens. "I am as healthy as any other woman—perhaps healthier, because of my studies. But I cannot marry you, signor. I must finish my examinations. I've come too far to stop now." I turn with a pleading look to Uncle Dante's lawyer. "My uncle would never approve of this."

The lawyer shakes his head, unconcerned. "Everything has changed now. You won't be a physician. You'll be a wife, which is a far better thing for a woman."

My toes curl, my hands clench. This man does not feel any loyalty to me, it's clear. Very well. If he will not advocate for me, I must advocate for myself.

Standing tall, I lift my chin. "No. I refuse."

Signor Lucchesi's expression darkens into something molten and ugly. "I'll take this matter to court if I must. As

God is my witness, I won't hesitate to have you imprisoned for refusing to pay your debt, signorina."

Again, that tingling in my fingertips, an urge to strike his florid face.

I stand in silence for a long moment, struggling to calm my breath. Shaking, I regard the lawyer and somehow find my voice.

"There must be some other way for you to use the courts and the rule of law to help me settle the matter of my uncle's debt, signor."

A terrible silence falls. My stomach drops. Why won't he speak in my defense?

"Your uncle was indebted to me, too, signorina," the lawyer finally says, his expression stony. "Signor Lucchesi has been kind enough to pay off the debt in gold. It's safe to say my loyalty no longer lies with your family."

Signor Lucchesi takes a step toward me, eyes glittering with malice. Any hope I had that his hard demeanor concealed a streak of kindness disintegrates.

"Your faithful servant is counting on you." He points at the door. "What will become of her now? Will she stay at your side and be a maid to a merchant's wife, safe and well-fed for the rest of her days? Or will she be cast out on the streets, made to beg for scraps? Her fate lies in your hands. Sign, and she will live out her days with dignity."

Uncle Dante, how could you leave me in this horrible predicament? Why did you do this to me, to us?

The hateful thoughts race though my mind like wild, terrified horses.

Prison for me, a beggar's life for Rosetta? Unthinkable. That leaves me with only one option.

I long to flee, to take Rosetta and return to my life before Uncle Dante's death . . . to a time when I was a confident young woman preparing for my medical exams, assured of my place in the world.

No. I cannot run. I must face my fate.

All three men stand over me while I ink my name on the record book, agreeing to marry. Somehow I keep my hand from trembling as I scratch the words *Giuliana Rinaldi* on the page, my eyes burning with tears.

CHAPTER 6

I ADVANCE through the streets with long, purposeful strides. Rosetta takes two steps for every one of mine. I've never been so agitated. It feels as if ants are crawling over my skin. I want to scream. I want to explode. I want to demolish a stone wall, a building, the world.

"Why in the name of Santa Maria are we going to the harbor?" Rosetta demands. "There's no fish market today. No merchant fleets have come in. It'll be windy as the devil's breath. My eyes will water, my fingers will swell from all this walking . . ."

I ignore Rosetta's complaints, outrage still boiling in my veins. I march as fast as I can toward the sea. The shifting waves beckon with the promise of distant shores, places where I could vanish forever, elude Signor Lucchesi and his notary for good.

The familiar streets of Salerno are a prison now, Uncle Dante's home a holding pen. I am burning to escape the only place I've ever known. How could my beloved uncle have put me in this position? He's never done anything even slightly questionable before. And now—*this*?

After my parents died, Uncle Dante was a father to me. He'd ensured my path to medical school was smooth. All I wanted was to be a physician. That was my future.

But now his enormous debt is pressing down on my shoulders like a slab of granite, grinding my dreams into dust. And a smug stranger is about to purchase me like a broodmare, expecting me to do nothing more than bear his children and run his household.

"No!" I say aloud, regretting the moment I'd put quill to paper. "I won't!"

"What's that?" Rosetta draws abreast of me, panting. "What won't you do?" she asks, her eyes bright with curiosity.

I force away the swirl of dark thoughts. "Never mind."

We pass through the city gates, the guards barely giving us a glance. The breeze coming off the harbor is cool, and I gulp the air as if it's water, grateful to have put space between myself and the lawyer's office.

"Look into a gull's cold yellow eyes, and you'll see the devil staring back at you," Rosetta mutters with a frown, staring at a seabird overhead.

Several merchant galleys shift and creak in the gentle swells. The Basque vessel is still here, its strange black-and-white banners rippling in the breeze. Another boat displays two yellow-and-red flags that identify it as Catalan. My gaze settles on the white-and-red banners atop the masts of a third galley, the one my uncle had remarked upon the day he died. It's now clear to me that this ship belongs to Signor Lucchesi. In a few days, I will be forced to board the vessel at his side, destined for a future as a merchant's wife.

I press my hands to my face, trying to calm myself. Anger is useless now. I must think of a solution to my problem. Somehow I must refuse Signor Lucchesi's marriage plan, to back out of the contract. It was stupid to sign the document. But what choice did I have?

My racing thoughts ease, and I begin to make a plan. Perhaps I can go to one of Uncle Dante's friends—there are a few lawyers among them—and find a way to break the contract.

As soon as I have the thought, a new realization strikes me like a hammer blow.

I can't stay in Salerno if I refuse to honor Signor Lucchesi's marriage contract. He already warned me of the outcome. He'll take everything, and I'll be thrown in debtors' prison. My only way out is to leave here before the wedding day and never come back.

But there is no other medical school equal to Salerno's. As a woman, I cannot complete my studies and achieve my certification anywhere but here. I will not become a physician now.

I heave, try to take a breath, and can only draw in the tiniest sip of air. My knees turn to jelly. The bright sun fades into pinpricks of light as darkness descends.

"God in heaven!" Rosetta cries. "What's the matter?"

I steady myself by breathing deeply and regarding each anchored vessel in turn, silently naming the colors on their banners. With effort, I push away my emotions. I must think logically.

My gaze settles on the Basque ship. Crewmen move about the deck, singing as they work. I remember the captain's name—Eneko—and the debt of gratitude he said he owed my uncle. A desperate idea takes shape in my mind as I watch the ship's banners shudder in the wind.

"What are you staring at, signorina?" Rosetta demands. "First, you nearly faint dead away, and now you're silent as a ghost. You're frightening me, by the saints!"

"Rosetta." I turn to her and put my trembling hands on her shoulders. "All will be well. Stop your worrying. Do you hear me?"

She looks taken aback, but she stops talking.

I survey the dock and see a pair of "wharf rats"—boys of about ten who run errands in the harbor—trotting toward us.

"Boys!" I call out. "Do you have a boat?"

The taller of the two puffs up his chest. "Of course! Can't work the docks without a boat!"

"No need to take that rude tone," Rosetta scolds.

"I'll give you a silver coin if you fetch the captain of that Basque ship for me," I tell him.

Rosetta turns to me in astonishment. "Is your mind addled, signorina? Those men could be pirates!"

The boys are already running toward their tiny craft, racing one another to be first aboard.

"Uncle Dante told me these Basques are men of good character," I say. "That should ease your worries, Rosetta."

"He always was too trusting, God rest his soul," she grumbles.

Shortly the boys return, their bobbing dinghy followed by a larger *grippo*.

I toss the taller boy a coin, and the pair of them dash off, chattering about roasted chestnuts.

Heavy footsteps pound the dock as the Basque captain and a companion approach.

"Signorina Giuliana," he greets me, his expression softening with a smile that strikes me as almost shy. "It's a pleasure to see you again."

"Captain Eneko," I return.

Suddenly, the audacity of my actions strikes me dumb. I've called him here, and now I can think of nothing to say. I struggle to find my voice, to put my plan into words without alarming Rosetta.

Unnerved by my silence, Rosetta puts a protective arm around my waist and eyes the captain with suspicion.

"Why do you speak in such a familiar fashion to my mistress, Basqueman?"

"I helped the signorina when her uncle died."

He puts a hand over his heart as he speaks, looking somber. I wonder if I'd imagined the smile a moment ago. Would a man like him let anyone, let alone a woman, witness a moment's vulnerability in his expression?

"Captain Eneko came to our home once, Rosetta," I say. "He and his men were injured and Uncle Dante helped them."

Her eyes widen. "That was you? Such a mess you made! All my linens bloodied, and so much water to boil for the professore's remedies."

"I am grateful for your help, Signora Rosetta," he says. "Every one of us survived, and you had a hand in that."

Rosetta tosses her head, pleased. "It's signorina, if you please, Basqueman. The embroidery on your shirt—is it your family's mark, that pattern?"

"You know something of my people," he answers, nodding. "Yes." Around his neck hangs a silver ornament stamped with the same pattern as his shirt. "I carry my family with me everywhere I go."

There is an earnestness in his tone, the same reverence he showed when he allowed Uncle Dante to cradle his head. Something in his manner makes my strength return, and with it, my resolve.

"When do you leave Salerno, Captain Eneko?" I ask.

"My ship is ready to sail, and I'm eager to get back to sea. But I'm awaiting cargo that hasn't arrived yet. I pray that it comes tonight, and we can be on our way in the morning."

"Where will you go next?"

"South."

A stab of disappointment makes me hesitate. I'd harbored a sliver of hope that he'd be heading north to Genoa. But there are dozens of other port cities strung like pearls on silk along the shipping routes in the Mediterranean. These ships could be destined for anywhere.

"A Genoan galley is anchored here," I persist. "Do you know if it returns to its home port soon?"

He shakes his head. "That ship is headed west. But I heard the captain of the Catalan ship say he was going to Genoa next."

"When is he leaving?"

"At first light tomorrow. At least that's what he claimed in a tavern after several cups of wine last night. Said he'd be laying in supplies for the journey today. Salted fish, biscuit, wine. He's somewhere in the city as we speak."

I take that in, my mind working furiously. I could be on a ship to Genoa tomorrow. Glancing at Rosetta, I know two things: whatever unfolds, she'll be at my side—and she won't be happy about the journey. But there's no better choice. The Catalan ship offers a chance to control my own destiny. If I don't take this opportunity, I'll never forgive myself.

"I'd like to meet with the Catalan," I say after a moment. "I have something of Uncle Dante's that he wanted me to give to his sister in Genoa. If I can get it to her, his dying wish will be granted."

Captain Eneko's brow lifts, then he gives a slow nod. "I need to purchase supplies in the city myself. I'd be glad to help you find the Catalan."

"It's not proper!" Rosetta looks scandalized. "Everyone says the Basque seamen are pirates."

"Not quite everyone, Signorina Rosetta," he says quietly.

I square my shoulders, searching his eyes with intense focus, as if by staring I can ferret out his true character. The truth is I've set this plan in motion and I need his help to see it through. Uncle Dante thought he was a respectable man. And, odd as it seems, I don't fear him—even if I should.

"We'd be pleased to accompany you, Captain Eneko." I point my feet toward the gates. "Let's be off."

CHAPTER 7

I AM up all night preparing for the journey while Rosetta sleeps in contented oblivion. When Captain Eneko introduced me to the Catalan in the marketplace earlier, I sent Rosetta to a nearby olive merchant's stall, so I could conduct the interaction without her knowledge, and kept my cloak's hood low over my forehead to avoid being recognized by anyone with an interest in my predicament. After we'd come to an agreement, Captain Eneko promised he would meet us at the harbor at dawn and ferry us to the Catalan's ship in his grippo.

During my brief encounter with the Catalan, neither his gaze nor his gait was quite steady enough for my liking. But he plans to leave Salerno tomorrow morning, and he's headed to Genoa.

This is my chance. My only chance. I must take it.

I roll up a few underthings and my extra cloak for use as a blanket, then put them in my satchel along with a small sewing kit, and a pot of the herbal ointment Uncle Dante swore by as a cure-all for aches, scrapes, and rashes. After a moment's reflection, I add the last of the medicinal herbs in our cupboards.

Next, I wrap Trotula de Ruggiero's book in waxed canvas and settle it alongside my cloak. I press my hand against my chest, reaching for the gold ring on its cord. I wonder briefly how many florins I could get by pawning it, then feel guilty for having the idea.

A pile of Aunt Amalia's letters tied with a black velvet ribbon catches my eye. I long to take all of them but restrict myself to just one. In addition to the usual invitation to visit Genoa, it contains a sketch of the square where her home is located. Aunt Amalia's wool merchant husband must be a wealthy man indeed, for every building on the square is large and fine. One of them is so magnificent it looks like a palazzo.

I pick up a battered leather tube containing scrawled recipes for medicines Uncle Dante compiled over many years. I place it in the satchel alongside the cloak. These could prove valuable even if I never practice medicine.

Finally, I go to my uncle's writing desk, to the hidden space behind the shelf where he keeps his inkpot and quills. I fiddle with the false back of the shelf until it comes loose, then extricate a worn leather purse. I heft it in my hand, recalling Uncle Dante's words when he revealed this secret place to me the day I began my medical training.

"It's always wise to have a little coin stashed away somewhere private," he told me all those years ago. "Perhaps it will make the difference if you find yourself in a difficult spot one day."

I long for his presence with a deep, aching fervor. If he were here I'd say, "Yes, you were wise to show me your hidden purse. But there was no wisdom in you incurring a great debt and never telling me a word about it!"

Nothing about his money-borrowing makes sense. I asked

his closest friend, the physician who lives near the harbor, if he knew about Uncle Dante's debt. But my query prompted only surprise and bewilderment in the man, not the answers I sought.

I count twelve gold florins in the purse. Their weight is reassuring. These coins—and his will—are proof that Uncle Dante did not purposefully forsake me. He will not see me become a physician, but I can still honor him by using this money to create a meaningful life for myself.

And then I hear a rap at the front door.

CHAPTER 8

I PAD to the window nearest the door and peer into the lane through a crack in the shutter. Signor Lucchesi and his notary are standing in the torchlight. The notary extends his arm to rap again.

Why are they here? Have they learned of my plan? My heart pumps furiously against my ribs as I gather my things and move silently to Rosetta's bedside.

"Rosetta." I shake her arm. "Wake up. We're leaving."

Rosetta rouses herself, blinking in the candlelight. "Leaving for where? Nothing is open. Market day isn't till Thursday. Church isn't till Sunday. Your wedding isn't till—"

There is another rap at the front door, louder this time.

"Who's there?" Rosetta springs out of bed, her sleepiness chased away by fear. "Bandits? Pirates?"

I concoct a patchwork of lies and truth as I bustle her into her clothes.

"The wedding's been canceled, and Signor Lucchesi is angry. I don't dare open the door to him. You've no reason to worry, though, as my aunt wrote and invited us to live with her in Genoa."

Rosetta stares at me in amazement, speechless for once.

"Put a few things in a satchel for the sea voyage," I continue. "Captain Eneko, the Basque, is meeting us at the docks at dawn. He'll ferry us to the Catalan ship. It's not far to Genoa, a week or so. You won't need much, for Aunt Amalia will see to our every need once we get there."

Rosetta looks doubtful as she gathers her personal items. "A sea voyage! What about my linens and my bed? I'd be a fool to leave those behind."

"You'll have a bed in Genoa. I promise." I shepherd her out the kitchen door, and we slip into the alley behind the house.

Overhead, the stars fade as the sky brightens. Dawn is coming.

A black cat startles from a doorway and darts across our path.

Rosetta gasps. "It's an ill omen, signorina! I've never been at sea, and I've never wished to be. Why must we go? You'd have a fine life as a wife to that merchant."

I pull her forward. "Signor Lucchesi did not want to take you in. I dared not tell you. It was too upsetting." The cruel truth tastes bitter on my tongue, as if I'm deliberately hurting her. "You'd be out on the streets if we were to stay here."

"Devil take him, then. You'll do us both a favor getting us to Genoa."

She stomps along, muttering about the loose sole on her left shoe that will trip her any moment, and the stitch in her side that will flare up if she goes any faster on these blasted cobbles, and the toothache that has been threatening to erupt in her jaw since last week.

"Less talking, more walking," I toss over my shoulder. "We must speed our steps."

We enter a nearby square. A group of servants carrying jugs

to the square's central fountain passes by, arguing about the size of a goat they'd seen on market day. Several pigeons peck aimlessly at the cobbles. As we leave the square, I glance behind us and see a pair of men hurrying from the alley we just exited.

With a lurch of panic, I recognize them as Signor Lucchesi and his notary. My pulse quickening, I urge Rosetta on.

At the gates, we wait for the changing of the guard. I shift my weight from one foot to the other as the on-duty guards greet the relief men and give their report to the captain. The guards fiddle with their swords and scabbards, then take their positions. One of them gestures us through the gates with a disinterested wave of his gloved hand.

A few dozen paces along the dock, I see a boat bobbing in the swells. A man is rowing it toward us, and another sits in the stern, a coil of rope in his outstretched arm.

"Signorina!" The man holding the rope waves. It's Captain Eneko.

He loops the rope over a post on the dock and clambers up a ladder, then bows to us.

"A calm day dawns. With enough breeze to take you on your way. Shall we go?"

A shout in the distance startles me. I whirl and see two figures weaving in our direction through the people and cargo on the dock.

"Yes!" I say quickly. "Let's go."

Captain Eneko helps us into the small craft, and we take our seats on a bench. He unhooks the rope from the dock and pushes off from the wooden pier while his companion dips his oars into the water, ready to row.

"Stop!" a voice commands from the dock. Signor Lucchesi and the notary stand waving their arms, indicating we should return.

"That woman is betrothed to me," Signor Lucchesi cries. "Our wedding is next week!"

Captain Eneko gives me a startled look. "Is this true?" he asks.

My stomach clenches. Rosetta begins to weep.

I take a shuddering breath, sure the Basques will turn the boat around. They'll give us to these men and condemn me to a fate I do not want.

"I will not marry," I say leadenly, fearing the worst.

The bleakness that descends over me as I utter the words must show on my face, for Captain Eneko turns and calls out, "You have the wrong lady." He says something in rapid Basque to his companion, and the little boat glides swiftly away from the dock.

The wool merchant shouts at us again, his angry voice fading with every oar stroke.

Gratitude wells up in my chest, warming my body, reigniting hope. I am giddy with relief and exhaustion. I turn to Captain Eneko, searching for the right words to convey how much it means that he believed me, that he refused to obey the man's command.

"Thank you," I say in a voice so faint it's practically a whisper.

Without speaking, he holds my gaze a moment, and in his eyes is a look of raw, genuine sympathy.

CHAPTER 9

Captain Eneko helps us climb aboard the Catalan galley. As he leads us to the captain, I throw nervous glances at the harbor. What if Signor Lucchesi sends someone in pursuit of us and my chance at freedom vanishes? With a pounding heart, I force myself to greet the captain.

"So the signorina is true to her word." He folds his arms over his chest, smiling. "I wondered yesterday if you'd appear, especially after that fellow questioned me about you."

"What fellow?" I ask, alarmed.

"A notary. Too inquisitive for my taste. He interrupted my snack, you see. I'd gotten a grilled squid, hot off the brazier at my favorite street vendor—"

"What did you tell him?" Captain Eneko's voice breaks in, steely and insistent.

The Catalan frowns at the interruption.

"I said the signorina had inquired about the journey to Genoa." He looks at me expectantly. "Didn't tell him you'd be aboard, though. As you hadn't paid me yet. So—do you have what you owe me?"

I dig into my purse and come up with three florins. It

seems an outrageous sum for a voyage that takes less than a week, but I have no alternative.

Two chickens run by, squawking furiously, pursued by an orange cat. The captain shouts for a cabin boy to collect the chickens, then peers at Rosetta.

"You didn't tell me you'd be bringing a companion," he says. "It'll be double for two passengers."

I resist an urge to protest. He'll order us off his ship if I refuse. But if I give him three more florins, my purse will be too light when I arrive in Genoa. What if Aunt Amalia is on a journey or cannot take us in for some reason? We must have money set aside for lodging and food if necessary.

Captain Eneko leans close to the Catalan and murmurs something to him.

The Catalan eyes Rosetta. "He says you can cook, signora."

Rosetta draws herself up proudly. "It's signorina, not signora. And of course I can cook! Better than any Catalan, I assure you."

"I'm short a cook, as it happens," he replies. "I could use you in the kitchen. What say you?"

I frown. "Will she be safe in your kitchen? Are they all men, the cooks?"

"Boys, more like it," says the Catalan dismissively. "They need someone to tell them what to do."

Rosetta rolls her eyes. "I've been telling kitchen waifs what to do since I was a slip of a girl."

"Make supper for the passengers tonight," he tells her. "I'll be the judge of your skill in the kitchen."

"If she's going to work for you, then pay her," I say. "And I'll give you nothing for her passage to Genoa."

The captain's expression tightens. "If her food is acceptable, you won't pay for her passage. But she won't earn anything either. It's a trade."

"When you taste my cooking, you'll want to pay me," Rosetta asserts. "That's a fact."

"If you're lying to me, you won't like the consequences." His gaze slides from Rosetta to me, and I don't like the speculative gleam in his eyes.

As the captain explains the kitchen duties to Rosetta, Eneko and I step away.

"She truly can cook, I hope?" He lifts an eyebrow.

I nod. "I only wish she weren't quite so blunt-spoken."

He grins, and the puckered scars on his cheeks vanish into deep laugh lines. A warm buzz of complicity and amusement thrums between us, buoying my mood. Then a strange melancholy seeps over me at the prospect of his absence, along with a prick of fear. I don't want him to leave.

"I'll not forget your kindness," I say, feeling awkward as the silence deepens.

He pulls a sheathed dagger from a leather bag slung over his shoulder and extends it toward me, squinting against the bright sunlight. "All travelers should be armed."

I draw aside my cloak to display my own blade.

"You carry a weapon?" he asks in surprise.

"I used to accompany my uncle on his rounds as part of my medical studies. He attended to the poor at no charge. We never knew what we would encounter in the streets. I only had to draw my blade once, for my uncle was respected by all in that city, no matter their circumstances."

"What happened on the day you wielded your blade?"

I shake my head. "It's a tale for another time."

"Fair enough. I wish you a safe voyage. May Santa Maria protect you—and may Mari, storm goddess of the Basques, keep you in her favor." He turns to go.

I stare at his retreating back as if in a trance. In all my dealings with men, whether they be my uncle's peers, my fellow students, or citizens of Salerno I encounter every day,

I've never felt so intrigued by any of them as I am by this Basque sea captain.

Our cabin is tiny, the "walls" made of waxed canvas, and it smells of mildew. Next to us is a merchant couple, and the wife's warm greeting makes my tense muscles ease. She tells me a common space provides a gathering spot for a single daily meal, and we'll receive hard biscuit, cheese, and wine to round out our rations.

I sit on the narrow wood-framed bed, its woven rope mattress digging into my flesh, and worry about Rosetta for a while. Finally, I spring up and make for the upper deck. At least in the salt air, I can breathe freely.

Long wooden oars jut from the hull, dipping and flashing in the sun. Crewmen range over the vessel, unfurling sails and lashing ropes. The insistent blasts of trumpeters heralding our passage to the open sea make my ears ache. I watch the tiled roofs of Salerno fade in the haze, praying Signor Lucchesi is not boarding another ship, intent on chasing us.

More chickens amble by, cackling.

"As long as the cat stays out of sight, you'll be safe," I tell them softly. "I know what it is to be pursued. And how good it feels to be free."

Crewmen adjust the ship's course, turning us in a slow arc to the north as a steady wind pushes us through the waves. Soon the oars are drawn into the galley's interior, accompanied by an intricate blast of the trumpets.

I silently thank Santa Maria for the wind speeding our progress. Every moment puts me farther away from a fate I did not want and did not deserve. For what feels like the thousandth time, I conduct an imagined conversation with Uncle Dante about his baffling debt and his failure to prepare me for it. My sweet uncle, my champion, my mentor . . . Why did he ignite this disastrous chain of events?

A surge of anger toward him heats my chest. Ashamed, I banish the thoughts, studying a mounted swivel gun on the deck with trepidation. Why would a merchant vessel need such a weapon?

The captain approaches. "We'll keep you safe, signorina. There's a gun on the starboard side, too. In case of pirates."

I turn, thinking of Eneko. Is he a pirate or not? We never settled the question to my satisfaction.

"Do you often see pirate ships?" I ask.

"Military ships are far more common than pirate vessels in these waters. But it never hurts to be prepared."

The captain strides off, dispensing orders as he goes. His curt demeanor reminds me uncomfortably of the wool merchant. Would Signor Lucchesi go so far as to pursue me to Genoa? I try to dismiss the idea. Why would he bother? He'll likely sell Uncle Dante's house and furnishings and be done with it.

I tell myself he'll soon find another wife. Fertile young women are plentiful, I know very well. They often came to Uncle Dante pregnant, unmarried, and desperate.

Trotula de Ruggiero made caring for such young women her life's work. That had been my goal as well. Until Uncle Dante died and my plans exploded like cannon shot.

A seabird following the galley drifts in a current of air above me. Rosetta fears seabirds as much as she fears crows, convinced they're spies doing the devil's work. But I see nothing evil in the bird's gleaming yellow eyes.

Once, Uncle Dante brought home the skeleton of an albatross found on the shore by some student of his. He explained how birds were able to fly not just because they had wings, but because their bones were hollow and light.

"Do you have any idea how fortunate you are?" I murmur

to the winged creature. "I was to be as skilled a physician as you are in flight. You're doing what you're meant to do. Will I ever have that chance?"

At this moment, my lifelong dream seems impossibly out of reach. I remind myself I'd be better served by concentrating on the present. Tomorrow is out of my control. Today is what matters. And Rosetta and I are vulnerable today.

Aunt Amalia has no idea I'm on my way to Genoa. If this ship sinks, if we're taken captive by pirates, if I contract the plague and die aboard the vessel, she'll never know. We are at the mercy of this Catalan captain, and his moodiness does not reassure me.

Though I've escaped marriage to Signor Lucchesi, I realize with no small measure of fear that my very existence now balances on the point of a blade.

Salerno shrinks in the distance as the wind pushes us north to the Tyrrhenian Sea. Beyond the city walls, the cathedral's curving dome glints in the morning light. Will I ever hear the clanging of its bells again? A burst of green marks the medical school's garden, where I spent countless hours harvesting leaves and roots alongside my classmates. Will I stroll along its gravel paths, breathe its herb-scented air once more? High above the city, Castello Arechi is the last to fade, its jutting turrets still visible as the coast falls away.

And then that, too, is gone.

CHAPTER 10

THAT EVENING, sitting on a stool shoulder to shoulder with other travelers around the supper table, I survey the meal with a smile. Rosetta has outdone herself. A lentil-and-sausage stew thick with garlic and herbs scents the air. A large platter of grilled squid is passed around and quickly emptied, as is a bowl of braised leeks and onions with fennel.

Sitting quietly, listening to the others, a feeling of pride unfurls in my chest. Several people comment on the tastiness of the stew and the squid, and I commit their remarks to memory so I can share them with Rosetta later. No one complains about the rations or the meal, though one merchant's wife says the watered wine is too heavy on the water. I take a long breath of relief, convinced the captain will hear only good reports about Rosetta's cooking.

Some of the passengers have brought musical instruments aboard, and after supper two lyre players and a tambourinist work their way through various nimbly performed melodies. I see a man slip away and return with a small keg from below decks. When it's passed to me, I pour wine into my ceramic cup and savor the rich, slightly fruity taste.

Though space is tight, some of the travelers begin dancing in time to the music. The others cheer them on, pounding their fists on the table. I tap my feet and clap along, admiring the movements of the dancers.

I never learned to dance, myself. Uncle Dante had no interest in dance. His time was spent caring for others, especially me.

The ship lists a bit as it crests a wave, and the dancers let out good-natured shouts, clutching one another for support.

Unnerved by the movement of the ship—for this is my first time at sea—I grasp the table with one hand and my cup with the other. I study the nicks and scars on the table's wooden slabs, observing the indentations of countless knives.

My mind slides to the future, to Genoa. If only there had been time to send Aunt Amalia a letter. What if my aunt is not even in Genoa? Her husband owns several galleys and has traveled to London and Flanders. Aunt Amalia once wrote of his longing to visit the Holy Land and her own desire to accompany him on a pilgrimage there.

It will be difficult, if not impossible, to set up a medical practice of my own in Genoa without proof of finishing my studies. I've no other skills that might lead to an income. I could work as a midwife, but Uncle Dante always warned me about the dangers faced by women healers whose knowledge is passed down from mothers and grandmothers rather than dispensed within the walls of Salerno's medical school. More and more, priests spread rumors of witchcraft and blame such women for births gone awry, stillborn babies, infants born with disfigurements.

Forcing myself to raise my chin, I turn my attention to the musicians, watch the tambourine flutter and the lyre strings vibrate.

The blare of trumpets on deck signals the end of supper-time. As the other passengers prepare to retire for the night,

I go in search of Rosetta. She must be finished with the supper chores by now, surely.

I make my way to the kitchen. I nearly laugh aloud when I see Rosetta with her sleeves rolled up and an immense linen apron tied around her midriff. She's holding court, ordering her helpers to wash, dry, stow, and scrub. The boys scurry to do her bidding, ducking out of the way of her well-placed pokes and jabs.

"You look like the queen of the ship, Rosetta," I tease.

Rosetta puts her hands on her hips. "They were hopeless when I arrived. Now they're learning. In two days, they'll be helpful. In a few years, one of them might be the master cook of a ship himself."

A boy turns at her words, his expression brightening.

"Master cook," he repeats, shaking his head. "That would be something."

"Don't get all dreamy now. Keep drying those kettles. And then wipe them out with a bit of oil so they don't rust."

Rosetta's crisp voice holds an undercurrent of kindness. The woman has a good heart, even if she is too blunt at times.

"I'll wait on deck until you're ready to go below," I say.

Rosetta gives me a distracted nod, immersed in latching the lids of various wooden tubs.

I step out of the kitchen to the deck, where the last fiery traces of the sunset illuminate the western horizon. The orange cat pads by, tail flicking. It eyes me for a moment, then continues on its way. Two cabin boys light the lanterns affixed to the masts, engrossed in conversation.

I lean my elbows on the deck rail and stare at the sky. A crescent moon glows overhead.

"It's a new moon. Always a good time to begin a voyage."

I turn at the captain's voice.

"Yes, that's what I've heard," I reply. "I'm glad to be traveling now."

"What takes you and your servant to Genoa, signorina?" His voice holds a trace of curiosity, nothing else.

Behind him, the flickering oil lamp casts shadows along the deck boards.

"I have family there."

"Have you been to Genoa before?"

I shake my head.

"It's a dangerous place," he says. "Full of scoundrels. And even if you manage to keep hold of your purse, everything there is more costly than it is in Salerno." He balances his elbows near mine, his gaze on the sea. "Travel can be so costly. But there are ways for women such as yourself—traveling without a chaperone—to earn money during the journey."

I regard him from the corner of my eye. "Mending sails?" I ask. "Braiding rope?"

He chuckles. "No, those tasks are best left to sailors."

With one swift movement, he slides closer to me and places a hand over mine.

"Every captain needs a woman to warm his bed." His voice is soft and cajoling in my ear, his breath foul and laced with wine fumes.

I jump as if he's stuck me with a pin and scramble away. He advances with a cocky little smile.

"How dare you?" A prickle of fear stirs at the base of my spine. "I am a respectable woman."

His expression hardens, and his hand flashes out, taking hold of my left wrist.

I jerk away. He tightens his grip. Under my cloak, my right hand slips to the dagger's hilt.

"Get back, you devil!" My voice cracks. "Let go or you'll regret it."

The captain slowly relinquishes me. There's just enough

lamplight to reveal the confidence on his face—and the calculation.

"You've got spirit," he says. "I always love taming a spirited wench."

He's done this before, I realize. He's gauging what kind of character I have. Hoping I'm as timid and gullible as those who have likely come before me.

The fear I'd felt a moment ago is displaced by cold anger. Yes, I'm young. Yes, I'm innocent in some ways. But this man has no idea what I've encountered alongside Uncle Dante in the rough streets and most desperate households of Salerno. I've witnessed the damage wrought by conniving, violent men on too many blameless girls and women. And I've drawn a man's blood to defend myself. My grip tightens on the dagger, but I keep it hidden.

"Touch me one more time, and I'll slit your throat." My mouth is so dry I can barely push the words out. "I swear it by all the saints."

"You might change your mind during the voyage. It's happened before." His smile returns. "You're always welcome in my bed, signorina. Don't forget it."

He spins on his heel and vanishes into the gloom.

CHAPTER 11

THE NEXT FEW NIGHTS, I'm careful to walk with other passengers to our cabin from the evening meal. I lie awake, clutching my dagger, until Rosetta returns from the kitchen. During the day, I stay close to a portly fabric merchant and his talkative wife, shadowing their movements along the deck and following them below when they take their afternoon rest.

When I encounter the captain above decks one windy afternoon, I avoid his gaze and ask the merchant about the merits of various types of wool.

"English wools are reputed to be the best, but that's up for debate." He strokes his beard thoughtfully. "For my part, I prefer the merino wool that comes from Aragón . . ."

A powerful gust of wind pushes me off balance. The merchant's wife tucks her arm firmly around mine, and for some odd reason tears burn in my eyes at the protective gesture. I lean on the woman, taking comfort in her solid bulk, imagining for a moment she is no stranger, but my own mother. Uncle Dante often reassured me that my parents loved me deeply, and my mother—his youngest sister—doted on me before a fever took her away from me forever.

"Your first word was 'Mamma,'" he'd tell me. "And that made her very proud. You are everything she hoped you'd be, *cara* Giuliana."

Later, after a satisfying supper of roast mutton layered with sea salt and herbs, I follow the couple below decks and return to my cabin. By the light of a small oil lamp, I go through my belongings to make sure everything is in order.

I whisper a prayer of thanks when I see Trotula's book in its waxed canvas covering, the leather tube containing Uncle Dante's writings, and Aunt Amalia's letter. On impulse, I slide the letter down the front of my bodice. It rests atop Uncle Dante's ring, which hangs around my neck on a leather cord.

Rosetta calls out from the other side of the door, and I unhook the rope knot that serves as a lock. She bursts into the tiny cabin and splays on the narrow bed, bringing the sharp scent of lavender with her. One of her arms is wrapped in a length of linen that bears a dark stain.

"Why do you smell of lavender?" I ask in trepidation as I unwrap the bandage to find a deep cut oozing blood.

"The herb mixture for the roast had lavender in it, so I had my helpers prepare the meat. One of them piled the mutton atop a butcher's knife, the fool, and it all slid off the table into me when the seas got choppy."

I bring the oil lamp closer and hold it up to Rosetta's face. A red rash spreads from her chin to her cheekbones. My heart sinks as I contemplate what's to come. Soon her nose will swell and the flesh around her eyes will pillow like rising dough. Though lavender is a curative that heals many ailments, it has the opposite effect on poor Rosetta.

"Thank the saints the knife didn't stab you in the belly." I rummage for a pot of ointment and a fresh strip of linen.

Rosetta scratches her chin. "Confounded itch never feels better after scratching, but the urge is too strong to ignore."

Her words are slurred, and I give her a sharp look.

"So you drank too much wine to dull the itch. Lucky for you, it's also numbed your pain." I rub soap on the linen until it foams. "Hold still while I wash the herb oils from your skin. After that, I'll stitch you up."

Rosetta shrinks away, mouth set in an irritable frown. "God's teeth, but you sound like your uncle when you take that tone with me. Go ahead. Torture me. But do it fast!"

I cleanse her arm, then find Uncle Dante's steel needle and stitch the wound closed with silk thread. She is surprisingly stoic during the process, a blessing for which I thank all the saints. After applying ointment and binding her arm with linen, I wash her face and wrap more linen around her hands.

"Now you won't scratch all night. Lie back again and close your eyes. It will improve by tomorrow. It always does."

But even as I say the words, I doubt them. This is the worst rash I've ever seen on her.

Once asleep, she thrashes and moans, striking me in the head and shoulders several times.

I resign myself to not sleeping all night. The usual worries creep into my brain, chattering like mice. What if a ship prowls the waves in the dark, searching for me? Will Signor Lucchesi track me to Genoa? Will I be jailed? Will I be put to death?

A jumble of noises interrupts my dark thoughts. Men's voices seep through the planks above my head. I hear footsteps striking wood, heavy objects scraping across the deck.

I sit up, my muscles tensing. Rosetta stirs and wakes.

A muddle of prayers, chatter, and weeping sweeps through the passengers' quarters.

"Another ship is alongside ours!" the merchant's wife cries from next door. "Pray that our captain keeps us safe!"

Dear God, has Signor Lucchesi found me?

"Pirates!" Rosetta screams. "I knew this would be a disaster. I knew we'd be murdered!"

I scramble to my feet. "Stand up, Rosetta. Put on your cloak and hood."

If anyone sees Rosetta's swollen face, they might suspect she has some disease. It's better to avoid such situations, I've learned. Most people do not care for explanations about the sensitivity of human skin and reactions to various substances. They only know swelling and rashes often lead to disfigurement—even death.

The makeshift canvas door shifts, the knotted rope straining against its wooden peg.

"Open up." The captain's tone is harsh.

"Why?" I say, remaining still.

"You're needed above decks."

"Who's asking for me?" I demand. "Is he a wool merchant? Is he Florentine?"

"Saints above, stop questioning me!" he splutters. "Open, or I'll slit this canvas with my blade."

Rosetta clings to the hem of my cloak. "Don't leave without me, signorina."

"Never," I promise her.

With trembling hands, I unlatch the rope knot. The captain regards me, stone-faced. Behind him, a cabin boy holds aloft a lamp.

"Come along. Speed your step." The captain wheels.

I follow on wobbly legs, my satchel slung over my shoulder. Rosetta follows, praying aloud to Santa Maria.

Above decks, the sky is molten amber in the east, the rising sun extinguishing the glimmering stars overhead.

A galley bobs in the swells nearby. I can just make out the banners flapping from its masts, emblazoned with Basque designs.

I stop, frozen by confusion.

The captain turns, eyeing Rosetta. "I don't know why you're bringing the cook, though. She stays with me."

"No, no!" Rosetta cries. "I'm going with the signorina."

"Don't be foolish, woman. I'm your master now."

I take Rosetta's hand. "We stay together."

A tall form looms beyond the captain. Taking in a quick breath, I recognize Eneko. That strange blend of longing and inexplicable familiarity seizes me at the sight of him, burning a path to my heart.

"I don't understand," I say. "Why are you—"

"Are you hurt?" He looks me up and down in apprehension.

I shake my head, and his expression eases slightly.

"Good," he says. "My grippo awaits." He inclines his head at a ladder leading over the side of the galley to the small boat below.

"But we're going north to Genoa!" I say, astonished. "You told me in Salerno that you were headed south, not north."

"Yes, yes." His tone sounds vague, as if he's simply placating me. "South first. Then north."

I fold my arms across my chest. "This makes no sense!"

"Nothing in life makes sense, signorina. You have to trust me."

An insistent flapping arises from a wooden crate nearby, followed by a strange high-pitched shriek. I flinch.

"Trust you? I barely know you."

He holds out a hand to me. "Please believe me when I say it was a mistake to put you on this ship."

All the air escapes from my lungs as I stare at his extended arm, grappling with my instincts. Of course we should flee. This is our chance to get away from the Catalan. But what will we encounter aboard the Basque ship? *Are* those men pirates? Will we become their captives? I look warily from the Catalan to Eneko. Finally, I decide to throw my lot in with the Basque and pray I'm making the right decision.

I take Eneko's hand, climbing onto the rope ladder, pressing the satchel against my body with my other arm. Below me, two Basque crewmen await in the grippo.

"Come," I order Rosetta. "Follow me and stay close—"

"The servant stays here," the Catalan cuts in.

Rosetta lunges for me. "No! I won't stay."

The Catalan stalks over and seizes Rosetta's arm, pulling her away.

"You're hurting me!" Rosetta squeezes my hand so tightly I let out a gasp.

A creature in the wooden crate shrieks again.

"Come now," Eneko cajoles the captain. "I've given you two rare saker falcons, a valuable gift. Let me keep this pair of women in return."

I take in a sharp breath. "You're trading us for . . . for *birds?*"

My leather soles slip on the flax rope ladder. I swing wildly, lose my grip on Rosetta's hand, and the satchel flies free of my arm. It lands in the black water in the narrow space between the grippo and the galley with an ominous splash.

"Santa Maria!" I cry.

A Basque crewman below leaps from one side of the grippo to the other, lunging for the satchel. Rosetta's screams tear my gaze away, and I crane my neck to see her entangled with the captain. Eneko is towering over them both, trying to negotiate with the man. With a strength I didn't know I possessed, I hoist myself backward and land awkwardly on the deck boards. All three of them look at me, startled.

I dart to Rosetta's side and tear back her hood, a wave of fury rising in me.

"Look at her!" I demand of the Catalan captain. "Do you truly want this creature cooking your passengers' meals? What fate will await you in Genoa if they fall sick and die because of her?"

He squints at Rosetta's misshapen face in the lamplight with a frown. "Is she sick? What ails her?"

"Do you want to keep her aboard or not?" I hiss the words at him.

Eneko steps to my side, his expression alarmed. "Wait. I don't want her aboard either—"

I sense his resolve wavering. The glimmer of Rosetta's wide, fearful eyes prods me to be bold.

Leaning close, I say, "Trust me."

He pauses for a beat, studying me with a long, measured stare.

"We'll take the woman with us," he says, turning to the Catalan. "No risk for you that way."

"Get yourselves off my ship, then, all of you." The Catalan's voice is icy. "Last time I do you a kindness, Basque."

CHAPTER 12

I HUDDLE next to Rosetta in the grippo, draping a protective arm around her shoulders. She fed me, held me when I was hurt, told me silly stories in ridiculous voices to make me laugh, and did countless other small but essential things to help Uncle Dante raise me over the years. Since his death, I feel as if our roles have been reversed.

At my feet, the satchel sits sodden and lumpish, its battered leather darkened by seawater. I can't bear to think about the contents, especially Trotula's book.

The little boat quickly closes the distance to Eneko's galley with its bold black-and-white banners rippling in the wind. When the rope ladder is unfurled for us, I pull Rosetta's hood low over her forehead and make her climb up first. She's fearful, but one of Eneko's crewmen—the fellow who rescued my satchel—calms her with a steady patter of encouragement.

"Follow me below," Eneko says once we're aboard. "You and Rosetta will bunk next to my quarters."

I look at him warily.

"There's a wooden door with an iron latch," he says, his manner softening. "You'll be safe."

Next to me, Rosetta trails along mutely, her head bowed. She's usually so lively, impossible to keep quiet. It's unsettling, seeing her like this.

"I said I'd trust you. But are we any safer here than aboard the Catalan's ship?" I demand as we descend below decks.

The smells of brine, sodden timber, and sweat are thick in the dim light. My satchel slaps against me as I walk, scattering droplets of seawater on the floorboards.

He waves us into a tiny cabin, then meets my gaze. "After you sailed away, I met someone who informed me the Catalan preys on young women like yourself."

I nod slowly, a cold feeling settling in my chest. How much longer could I have avoided the Catalan's advances? I'd been in danger, perhaps more than I cared to admit.

"Who told you that?" I ask, still wary.

"A woman." He rubs his hand over his beard. "She told me the Catalan robbed her of her virtue on his ship."

Rosetta gasps.

"What happened to her?" I ask.

"She bore his child, then she was cast out by her guardian. She had no choice but to prostitute herself. I could not abide sending you to the same fate."

As Eneko tells his tale, I lose track of his words, imagining what could have happened if the Basques had not removed us from that ship. What if I'd tried to fight off the Catalan and failed? What if I had been raped, impregnated by that devil—

I take several deep breaths, forcing my attention back to Eneko.

"My cargo arrived in Salerno harbor the very next day," he is saying, "so we left in haste and tracked the Catalan's ship with ease. All merchant ships follow the same routes up the coast to Genoa, and my galley is much faster than his."

"Those falcons were the cargo you needed?" I ask.

He nods. "I'd learned a trader from Crete would be coming to Salerno with a load of saker falcons; that's why we dropped anchor there. Believe me, I'd no desire to return to the city after our last misadventure. Once I had the falcons, I made haste to overtake the Catalan. I'd put you in harm's way, and it was my intention to remove you from any danger. It's the least I can do to repay my debt to your uncle."

Rosetta's spirit returns with a sudden, blaring question. "But are you pirates or not? Tell us the truth and be done with it."

Eneko turns his gaze on her. She's a sorry sight. Face swollen as an overripe plum, dotted with an oozing red rash.

"Just about every ship at sea is full of pirates, in my experience. Some seamen are born pirates; some become pirates against their will." His voice is sober, without a trace of mockery or merriment. "Men who call themselves privateers are hired pirates, paid by the doge of Venice or the Great Council of Genoa or the Knights Hospitaller of Rhodes. Others work for themselves, mostly to provide for their families."

I take that in. "And which kind of pirate are you?"

He half smiles, and his eyes gleam at me in the shadowy light.

Rosetta crosses herself. "I knew it! God help me. I'd rather be on that Catalan vessel, slathered in lavender, blistered from head to toe, as Santa Maria is my witness!"

I turn to her. "The Catalan captain wanted to make me his whore, Rosetta. If we'd stayed aboard, he might have succeeded. Now we'll sail to Genoa with the Basques. We'll soon be lodged with my aunt."

Eneko clears his throat. "We have a small matter to attend to in Malta first."

I clench my fists. "Malta?"

"I told you we're heading south."

"How far south is Malta?"

He shifts his weight, looking uncomfortable. "Ten days, if the wind's with us. I'll get you to Genoa—I vow it. But I'm beholden to someone in Malta, and we're all at risk if I don't deliver him the goods I've promised."

Rosetta flings herself down on the bed, praying aloud to Santa Maria, God, and all the saints to protect her.

Suddenly, I'm exasperated with Rosetta's dramatic moods. She's distracted me from my waterlogged satchel for too long. Ignoring her, I sink to my knees and unbuckle the wet, swollen straps.

To my surprise, Eneko crouches at my side. "How bad is it?"

Gingerly, I extract the roll of papers. The leather case is soaked, and the cover is difficult to remove. With tentative movements, I withdraw the contents. The outer pages are damp and the ink illegible in parts, stained by seawater. But the inner rolls have survived nearly intact.

"This is better than I expected," I admit, digging for the book. The canvas cover is wet. I unwrap the cover and carefully open it. The linen pages cling to one another, clammy under my fingertips. With infinite care I tease apart two pages. I suck in a breath, shocked. The words have copied themselves on the opposite pages, obscuring the original inking with illegible gibberish.

"Oh no." I experiment with pages midway through the book, then near the end. All of them exhibit the same damage. Trotula's book is ruined. At the sight, the hope I'd entertained about practicing as a physician specializing in women's ailments flickers like a guttering candle, then vanishes. It feels as if my spine has turned to mush. I slump over the book, head bowed.

Rosetta's warm hand squeezes my shoulder. "Your uncle's precious book. He'd roll in his grave to know what's become of it."

Eneko rocks back on his heels. "What's so important about the book?" His tone is respectful.

"It contains the teachings of a woman physician from Salerno."

"The greatest physician ever born," Rosetta adds stoutly. "Trotula de Ruggiero."

"Healer, you mean?" Eneko asks. "I've not been acquainted with any women physicians, but Basque country's got many woman healers whose wisdom isn't written in the pages of books."

"She was a physician," I tell him. "She went to the Schola Medica Salernitana, where Uncle Dante taught. I am—I was —a student there."

He nods slowly, absorbing my words.

"You were to be a physician," he says quietly.

"Yes. My uncle's death changed everything. I wasn't able to finish my studies."

"There's no school in Genoa?" he asks.

I shake my head. "Salerno's school is unique in the world. It once admitted many women and employed female professors, but fewer and fewer women are permitted to enter its ranks. I was lucky. Uncle Dante's influence got me a place there."

"He always said the signorina was just as brilliant as Trotula," Rosetta puts in. "He said his niece deserved her schooling more than most of the men at the school."

I smile at Rosetta. Her loyalty shines through at difficult moments, and I'm grateful for it.

"That man in Salerno—the one who tried to stop you

leaving, who said you were his betrothed?" Eneko's question hangs in the air between us, and I put up a warning finger lest Rosetta fill the silence with her own version of events.

"He's a wool merchant from Florence. I don't know why, but Uncle Dante borrowed an enormous sum of florins over the years from the man and never told me. As I could not repay it, Signor Lucchesi demanded I marry him."

"He can demand anything he wants, but if you're not legally bound to him . . ."

I drop my gaze, overcome by a mixture of shame and regret. The more time passes, the more I chastise myself for signing that betrothal agreement.

"You *are* bound to him, then?" Eneko guesses.

"I signed something." I sigh. "He was threatening me and Rosetta. I was trapped."

Eneko rises and runs a hand through his hair. "And he thinks you're headed to Genoa."

"I am headed to Genoa!"

"Does your aunt know you're on your way?"

"She'll always welcome me. I have no doubt on that account." I stand abruptly, feeling defensive now.

"It's up to the fates whether the wool merchant pursues the matter," Eneko says. "But it's within his rights to take this to the courts if he ever finds you again. You'll have to be on guard every moment once you arrive in Genoa."

His expression unreadable, he walks out the door.

CHAPTER 13

ENEKO LEADS me to the bow of the galley on a sunny morning exactly ten days after he boarded the Catalan's ship. I squint against the light, watching the honey-gold cliffs of Malta rise up before us. A massive stone tower looms atop the highest cliff, its austere facade broken only by arrow slits. Foam-capped waves pound against the rocks, sending arcs of glittering sea spray into the air. Ahead, calmer waters create a natural harbor, where I can make out the dark shapes of anchored ships.

"You were right," I admit. "You said it should take ten days to get here, and it has."

He grins. "I prayed day and night for favorable winds. I'm glad you're pleased."

"Pleased?" I throw him a dark look. "I'd be pleased if we were sailing to Genoa. I have no business in Malta. But now that we're here, I'll take advantage of the time on land to find a remedy for Rosetta's arm. I removed the stitches a few days ago, but the flesh isn't healing as it should. I need herbs from an apothecary and fresh nettles to treat the wound properly."

I gesture at the arid cliffs surrounding us. "It may be more difficult than I'd imagined."

"But my crewman told me her spirits improve by the day," Eneko replies, frowning a little.

He has confined her to the cabin to keep her out of the crew's sight, though the sailor who helped her aboard the ship, Beñat, brings her daily deliveries of food and wine.

"Your man Beñat never fails to make her smile, but that doesn't improve the condition of her arm."

"We're going to a place called Mdina, far inland. You'll find gardens and apothecaries there." He glances at the sun. "We'll arrive well before dark, and you'll have comfortable lodgings in a fine home."

His skin is burnished copper-brown by the sun, save for the puckered, silver-white scars. The line of his jaw is solid and pleasing beneath his short beard. I imagine running my fingertips along it, following the angle of it with my lips. I've kissed two young men in my life, both students at the medical school, and I never noticed the angles of their jawlines. The thought sends heat to my cheeks.

"Whose home will we stay in?" I look away, hoping he won't notice the flush on my face.

"Signor Tarrag, a rich merchant who's eager for his gift of falcons." Eneko jerks his head toward the stern, where the falcon cages sit under a shade of waxed canvas.

"Why must you pay tribute to him?" I ask.

"The seas around Malta are dominated by his ships. They patrol the waters between here and Sicily and also south to Africa. There are few things more precious to a man who craves power than falcons. They're like a tax, a way to stay in his good favor and ensure safe passage."

"What would happen if you didn't bring a gift each year?"

"His ships would no longer see my galley as friendly. Since we don't often travel in a fleet, we're vulnerable when hostile ships approach. It would be foolish—and dangerous—to make an enemy of him."

The navigator calls out a question and Eneko excuses himself.

As I watch him stride off, a tingling warmth travels through my limbs like a thousand tiny shooting stars are lighting me from within.

Eneko's men procure a wagon, mules, and horses from an inn near the harbor, and it seems that no sooner are my feet on solid ground than I'm in motion again, rolling across the windswept plains of Malta. Next to me on the wagon bench, Rosetta sits arrow-straight, her eyes on Eneko and the two men riding alongside him. One of them is Beñat, who'd handed her up into the wagon with the deference and care of a royal servant to his queen. At one point he turns and raises a hand, smiling at her, and she returns the gesture with enthusiasm.

"That's a kind man, isn't it?" she says, clucking her tongue appreciatively. "He may be a pirate, but his mother raised him right."

As we approach the fortified city of Mdina, cultivated fields appear, interspersed with vineyards. After a slow climb up a gradually inclining hillside road, the wagon groans to a halt before the massive walls of the city.

"Look at that!" Rosetta cries. "A moat as deep as a lake. And a drawbridge shut up as tight as a clamshell. Will they let us in, do you think?"

Eneko shouts something to the guards atop the high walls and gestures at the wagon. I look over my shoulder at the cages strapped into the wagon's cargo area, draped with canvas. Both of the falcons within wear leather hoods to blind them for the journey, and neither of them have made a sound during the ride from the harbor.

Rosetta nudges me. "What if those precious falcons are dead? What if we're blamed for it?"

I look at her. "You truly love imagining the worst, don't you?"

"Perhaps I should rap on their cages, to check—" She extends an arm, the wounded one, and flinches. "Shouldn't have done that. It hurts worse today than yesterday, signorina."

Slowly, the great drawbridge is lowered, meeting the earth with a dull thud.

All I can think of is Eneko's promise that I'll find the medical supplies I need within these walls.

We pass through cramped streets and enter a broad, sunny square dominated by a church with a soaring bell tower. Well-dressed citizens stop to stare at our wagon and the mounted men. I clench my jaw, uneasy at the scrutiny.

Halfway across the square, three armed men in light-colored tunics emerge from an alleyway. The man at the center of the group puts a hand to his heart and bows.

"Welcome to the Cítá Notabile, the Noble City," he says. "My master summons you to his residence."

Eneko says something in response that I can't hear, and a brief conversation ensues. We follow the men into a lane bordered by lovely stone facades with iron-studded wooden doors. Beñat and the other Basques enter a broad open doorway that leads to an inn of some kind. The wagon driver follows our guides a bit farther down the lane, then we roll into the lofty courtyard of a grand residence.

I take in delicately carved stone balconies, ceramic planters spilling over with lush flowers and fruit trees, water spouting from a marble fish's mouth in a shimmering pool.

A thickset, heavily bearded man in a white silk tunic

appears from the central doorway of the residence, arms outstretched in greeting. He crosses to Eneko as the Basque dismounts, and they embrace in the way of old friends.

Then he approaches the wagon and offers me his hand. I accept it and descend, grateful to be on firm ground again.

"I am Signor Tarrag, merchant of Mdina. But you are exquisite!" He claps his hands together, smiling in delight. "Eneko never told me he had a companion of such beauty."

I'm a bit unsettled by his enthusiasm, not to mention his choice of words. "I'm not—we're not—"

"Signorina Giuliana's family has put her under my protection," Eneko asserts, appearing around the side of the wagon.

"Ah!" The man nods sagely, eyes sliding from Eneko to me. "As you say. Welcome, signorina."

Eneko helps Rosetta from her perch, and she turns in a circle, mouth agape, taking in the beauty of the courtyard.

"My servant has a wound that needs tending," I tell Signor Tarrag. "Perhaps your kitchen garden has the remedy. And I'll need to visit an apothecary."

"Of course, of course," our host says. "My servants will instruct you. First, you'll be taken to your chamber. Never fear, you'll be well cared for here."

We follow a servant inside. As Rosetta falls into step alongside me, she whispers, "I fear for those falcons. Not a peep from either of them. Doesn't bode well, if you ask me."

"It's not our business whether they're alive or dead. There's nothing we can do about it."

Rosetta crosses herself, her mouth moving in silent prayer.

The cool interior of the home offers a welcome respite from the harsh sunlight. At the end of a wide corridor, the woman gestures us into a chamber dominated by a carved wooden bed. The shutters on the two windows opposite the bed are thrown open, admitting light from a small courtyard brimming with jasmine, pomegranate trees, and lemon trees. A small table holds a pitcher of wine and a plate of apricots and almonds.

"You'll be taken to the bathhouse before supper," the servant tells us. To Rosetta, she adds, "You can come to the kitchens with me after your bath."

Rosetta draws herself up. "To work?"

The woman shakes her head, smiling. "To eat. With the other servants."

I look at Rosetta's bandaged arm, frowning. Before anything else, we need to tend to her wound.

"First, I need hot water and soap brought here, along with clean linen for bandages and nettles from the kitchen garden," I tell Signor Tarrag's servant. Then I turn to Rosetta. "You go along with her and harvest the nettle leaves, then ask the cook for a mortar and pestle, salt, and vinegar. We'll prepare the remedy here."

In Salerno, Rosetta often accompanied me to the medical school's garden and helped me harvest herbs. I know she'll get exactly what I need.

I press a handful of almonds in Rosetta's palm, and she follows the servant out the door.

Another young female servant enters, carrying a red silk gown and fine cotton underclothes.

"For this evening," she says, laying the items carefully on the bed.

I look ruefully at my brown wool dress, which bears the evidence of a sea journey and a dusty ride.

"I'm grateful to Signor Tarrag," I say. "I have no other clothes."

"It was Signora Tarrag, not the signor, who told me to bring you these things."

Her voice holds a trace of sharpness. As the words linger in the air between us, I see the unmistakable shadow of a bruise on her cheekbone. Looking closer, I realize her lower lip is healing from a cut.

"You're hurt," I say softly.

The servant's arms tighten around the towels.

"I'm trained to help women with their injuries and illnesses," I continue. "As soon as I visit an apothecary, I'll get the remedies I need to treat your pain."

She looks at me with wary amazement. After a moment's hesitation, she turns away, vanishing through the door on quiet feet.

A thought plagues me the rest of the afternoon: Who is beating that young woman, and why?

CHAPTER 14

SURROUNDED by a buzz of conversation in the *sala nobile*, a spacious chamber with high ceilings, I take in the colorful tiled floor, the massive olive wood table in the center of the chamber, the silver oil lamps affixed to the walls. I've never been in such a grand space.

About a dozen other people mill about, greeting one another with familiarity. Eneko is immersed in chatter with a slender woman whose large, haunting dark eyes dominate her face. She wears an exquisite white silk gown edged with gold thread, her black hair mostly obscured by a flowing headpiece.

For his part, Eneko wears a dun-colored silk tunic over white cotton leggings, his long hair neatly pulled back from his face by a leather cord. I study his high cheekbones and wide mouth, admiring the symmetry of his features. The puckered, silvery lines of his scars are no longer jarring to me. He looks like a confident, starkly handsome man who has survived more than his share of danger and bears the marks of it. He catches my eye, and I drop my gaze, feeling vaguely guilty to have been staring at him.

A hush settles over the group as Signor Tarrag enters the room flanked by two personal guards wearing curved swords. He spreads his arms wide, calling out greetings to his guests. One by one, the gathered people bow to him as he passes by. The woman in white leaves Eneko's side and joins Signor Tarrag. My heart pumps faster as I realize the pair is approaching me.

"Signorina, allow me to present my wife. *Amore*, Captain Eneko was considerate enough to bring a beautiful companion, who will share all the news of Salerno with us this evening."

"My gown suits you." Signora Tarrag gives me a polite smile, but her eyes are cool. Now that she's an arm's length away, I realize she's much older than I first imagined, probably nearing forty. There's a tightness around her mouth, her brows are drawn together, and her posture is unnaturally erect. She's either very tense or in pain.

"Thank you, signora," I reply, running a hand over the soft silk of my skirts. "I'm grateful for the loan. It's very kind of you."

"It is not a loan, signorina. The gown is my gift to you."

I look at her in surprise. "But, I cannot accept such a—"

She is already turning away, her gaze roaming over the assembled group, then settling on Eneko.

"You must sit next to me, signorina. I insist," Signor Tarrag says, tapping my shoulder. "Captain Eneko has had more than his share of your time. I've found him another companion for the evening."

He points at a rotund man dressed in pistachio-green silk who is approaching Eneko. But at that instant, Signora Tarrag returns to Eneko's side and leads him to a seat at the opposite end of the table, next to her own. She lifts her chin and gives her husband a triumphant look.

Signor Tarrag's expression tightens. As he shows me to my

seat, I cast a surreptitious glance at Eneko. He's sitting straight-backed in his chair, his mild expression revealing nothing. Signora Tarrag's hand is on his arm. Eneko said nothing of her to me on the journey here, but he has clearly met her before.

A group of musicians strike up a tune on their lutes and tambourines, interrupting my thoughts. The rest of the guests take their seats, and servants file in bearing silver platters heaped with grilled meats, fish, rice, vegetables, and fragrant sauces. A servant fills my plate with portions of every dish and pours sweetened white wine into my cup.

Signor Tarrag dips a chunk of flatbread in a dish of olive oil. "Tell me, signorina. Why did you leave Salerno, and where are you going to next?"

Down the table, his wife laughs at something Eneko said, covering her mouth with her hand. Signor Tarrag's attention darts to the two of them. A look of intense displeasure seizes his face. But it's gone so quickly that perhaps I imagined it.

"I travel to Genoa. I have an aunt there. My uncle died, so there was no reason to stay in Salerno."

"My condolences." Signor Tarrag pins me with a thoughtful gaze. "And what is your connection to Eneko?"

I hesitate, not sure how to respond. "Eneko knew my uncle," I say slowly. "He offered to be my chaperone on the journey to Genoa."

"Chaperone? Did your family pay him to escort you there?"

"Not exactly." My cheeks are growing hot. "I'm under his care. For my own safety, as I'm sure you understand. These sea voyages can be quite dangerous."

He sips from his cup. "Any journey is dangerous, whether overland or by sea. Particularly for young, unmarried ladies. My servants tell me you attended the medical school in Salerno. I wonder why you omitted that in your story, signorina. Few young women can say the same, after all."

I stiffen. "How did they learn of this?"

"Your own servant told them." He stares at me, looking smug.

I suppress a groan. *Rosetta.*

"I see," I say quietly.

"Yes, she said you have all the makings of a fine physician, just like your uncle, and you wish to cure the ailments of women." He chews a handful of pitted olives. "I shall send word to my associates in Genoa that their wives must call for you when they're ill."

Signora Tarrag's laughter rings out again. She is leaning close to Eneko, whispering in his ear. Eneko's smile looks unnatural. He normally seems comfortable in his own skin, but at this moment he looks as if he'd rather be anywhere else.

"My own wife will want to avail herself of your services." Signor Tarrag's voice is clipped now, his expression hard. "She has no end of complaints for me about her aches and pains. She saves all of her best moods for guests."

I reach for my wine cup, thrown off balance by his odd comment.

The musicians launch into a different melody, and Signor Tarrag's face lights up. "Ah! You must join us in the dance, signorina."

"I don't dance, signor."

"Nonsense! I won't allow anyone to sit while others dance. I consider it bad luck."

He stands, staring at me expectantly until I rise, and then signals to his wife to join him.

I submit to the scrutiny of the other guests at the table, uncomfortably aware that I am an outsider in this strange world. I twist my hands together, longing to be on Eneko's galley, gliding away from Malta with a powerful wind filling the sails.

To my relief, the others get to their feet and follow their hosts to the center of the space—all except for one man. I glance to the end of the table and meet Eneko's eyes. He slowly rises, draining his wine cup. Does he share my wish to be back at sea?

Signor Tarrag and his wife link hands and begin to dance. As the other guests follow suit, Eneko walks to my side and bows.

"You're glowing like a ruby," he says appreciatively. "Red suits you."

At his compliment, my skin tingles with pleasure. Instead of thanking him, I tell him I never learned to dance.

He looks unconcerned. "I'm a very good teacher."

He takes my hand. A dizzying heat flickers to life in my belly at his touch. I almost snatch my hand away as if I've been burned. But the heat suffusing my body is not painful; it's exciting. I keep hold of him, wanting to prolong the sensation.

He leads me to the others, who have formed a circle. They sway to the music, their arms held aloft, moving first to the right, then the left.

"See?" Eneko says. "Easy!"

I follow his movements as the tempo of the music increases, gaining enthusiasm with every step. My unsettled feeling ebbs away. Soon I'm smiling, breathless, tracing patterns on the stone floor with my feet. It's as if an invisible current connects me to Eneko, a force swirling around our bodies, keeping us linked together with a secret, joyous language understood by us alone.

The happiness on his face tells me he feels it, too.

When I catch Signora Tarrag's eye over Eneko's shoulder, the hostility on her face is like a deluge of icy water.

"Our hostess is watching," I tell him under my breath. "She does not look pleased. Perhaps you should dance with her next."

"To the contrary," he returns. "I'd rather keep my distance."

We mimic the other dancers, pressing our hands together palm to palm, then turning in a slow circle. Staring into his brown eyes at close range, I see flecks of gold glinting in their depths. His smile deepens, and it dazzles me. I breathe in his scent. A hint of rosemary fills my lungs, along with the faint scent of myrrh—a common aphrodisiac used by women and men alike.

"It could be your scent that's attracted her attention," I point out.

A muscle in his jaw flickers. "She's the one covered in myrrh oil. Her skin shines with it. I hate the stuff, myself."

"You seem to know her well," I say bluntly.

"When I was last here, she was a rich widow with a roving eye." His eyes narrow. "Things have changed."

I want to ask him why she's so familiar with him, but we're weaving between pairs of other dancers now, and there's no way to do it discreetly.

"How soon can we be on our way?" I ask when we're side by side again.

"I've paid my tribute to Signor Tarrag," he replies. "But he hasn't inspected the falcons personally yet. As soon as he does, we can leave. And, signorina, tell your servant to stop wagging her tongue. The less these people know about you, the better."

CHAPTER 15

I can't sleep that night. I lie awake on the soft bed in my chamber reimagining the evening's events. I can see the velvety night sky through the open windows, pulsing with stars. A trace of jasmine scents the air.

On her pallet in the corner, Rosetta snores softly. Before bed, I packed her wound with a fresh poultice of macerated nettles. She grumbled at the sting, but she knows as well as I do that nettles can stop infection before it kills.

I get up and pad to the windows, peering out at the darkened balconies across the way. Torches burn around the perimeter of the courtyard, illuminating the cobblestones with weak light.

A soft cry startles me. I see a slight form moving in the shadows, a woman. She's limping.

I tense. Is someone in this household beating all the female servants? I fetch my dagger, then slip into the corridor and down the spiral staircase to the courtyard, feeling my way through the darkness with one hand on the cool stone walls.

The torchlight gutters in the breeze. The shadows tangle and lengthen, clouding my vision.

Willing my heartbeat to subside, I follow the sound of weeping to its source. A young woman slumps against the wall by the fountain, her head buried in her arms.

I crouch by her. "What happened?"

She raises her chin. I realize this is the same servant who brought me towels and showed me to the bathhouse.

"I can taste blood on my lip," she says. "And my ankle hurts. I fell when he was chasing me."

"Who?"

"My master. I got away this time. I'm faster than him when he's drunk." She takes in a ragged breath, wraps her arms around her knees.

"Can you work in another house?"

She shakes her head. "He only hits me when he's angry at his wife. It could be worse. Besides, no one pays as well as him. And my family needs my wages."

My mind flits to the image of Signor Tarrag's furious expression when he watched his wife flirt with Eneko. I didn't imagine it, then. I wonder whether Signora Tarrag's own flesh bears the evidence of his anger, too.

"Let me help you." I offer a hand. "I can ease your pain, at least."

"I'm accustomed to pain." She stands without my assistance, and I know her moment of vulnerability is over.

As she melts into the darkness, I shake my head in frustration, all too familiar with her predicament.

I hear the slap of leather on stone, and I clutch the dagger tightly. A man approaches.

"Signorina Giuliana?"

I relax at the sound of Eneko's voice.

"What are you doing out here alone?" he demands.

"I heard a woman cry out. It was a servant. She—" I swallow the rest of my explanation. "Never mind."

"You must come with me," he says. "Signora Tarrag has called for you. She's ill."

We hasten through the dusky corridors to a large chamber where a buzz of activity is taking place. Lamplight spills from the doorway. Peeking inside, I see a woman lying on an ornately carved bed, surrounded by attendants. She's curled on her side, clutching her abdomen.

When I hesitate, he speaks again, low. "What can I do?"

"Don't leave me," I say. "No matter what happens."

I wish he would reach for my hand the way he did during the dance, entwine his fingers with mine. I long to feel the warmth of his touch, to take strength from him.

He searches my eyes, then simply says, "You have my word."

I go to Signora Tarrag's bedside. Her skin is ashy, and there are dark shadows under her eyes.

"You look like you're suffering," I say softly. "Is this pain new?"

"It started a few years ago. It's always in the left side, and it gets worse over time." She gestures at a set of bloodletting blades in a bowl near the bedside. "I hate my husband's physician. He studies my piss, reads the stars, gives me charms, and and bleeds me till I lose what little strength I have left. Your servant told my cook you're trained to cure women's ailments. Was she speaking the truth?"

"Yes." I hesitate. "Is Signor Tarrag home? Will he mind me examining you?"

"I don't give a whit if he minds."

She shoos her female attendants out the door and admonishes them to wait in the corridor with the guards.

"When it gets this bad, it brings on a headache that makes me vomit," she confesses. "Nothing helps but jusquiam. For pain and for sleep."

"Jusquiam?" I repeat. "Not poppy milk?"

"That's what I said," she snaps. "There's some in there." She jerks her head toward a small wooden cabinet near the bed.

I'll need to give her a different pain reliever. I would never administer a dose of jusquiam that's been concocted by someone else. The risks are too great.

I see no visible bruises on her, but I still ask if she has any other injuries.

She looks at me in surprise. "Injuries? What do you mean?"

"Some women are beaten by their husbands," I say evenly.

"My first husband was violent. But not this one. He wouldn't dare."

Her confidence is admirable. Signora Tarrag could be lying, but I sense she's telling me the truth. I take her pulse. It's a bit weak, but not alarmingly so.

"Have you birthed any children?" I ask her.

"Seven with my first husband. Five are dead. My two sons are at sea most of the time, may God and Santa Maria protect them."

I perform a basic examination and palpate her organs. Her left ovary is much larger than the other due to a tumor. She's having her monthly courses, and her menstrual cloth is soaked through with dark blood.

"Is this amount of blood normal for you?" I ask, changing the cloth.

"If a flood is normal for anyone, then yes."

I comb through my memories of Trotula's writings on the diseases of women and my uncle's illustrations of the female reproductive organs and their ailments. The ovarian growth could be harmless—or it could be cancerous. Regardless, its size is no doubt contributing to her pain.

Though Trotula's book is ruined, I've memorized a few important recipes, including one that reduces excessive menstrual bleeding. If I can collect all the ingredients tonight, I'll administer the remedy to Signora Tarrag.

"How is your appetite?" I ask her.

"Fine, fine." She waves a hand dismissively.

I take that as a good sign. If it were advanced cancer, she would not be much interested in food. "You have a mass in your ovary." I lay a hand on the affected area. "I can ease your pain and give you remedies that lighten the bleeding, but the pain will likely get worse as it grows larger."

She regards me with a faint look of astonishment. "You know all that just from touching my flesh?"

I nod.

"Go on, then," she groans. "Do what you can for me."

"I'll need pennyroyal oil, rose oil, and ground willow bark from an apothecary. I can make you a soothing elixir. And I'll need poppy milk, too."

She folds in on herself, pain furrowing her brow. "Tell the guards. They'll fetch it all."

"At this hour?"

"The apothecary is always in need of my gold, like most people in Mdina."

I go to the door and instruct the guards about the errand, then turn to the young attendants.

"Rouse the cook and have her make an infusion of nettle leaves with boiling water. We'll also need tea with dried chamomile and catswort."

The women hurry off to do my bidding.

"And bring clean linens for compresses," I call after them, "along with an extra bowl of hot water."

Near Eneko, an old female servant stands slump-shouldered by the door.

I fix her with a stare. "Can you tell a story? Sing a song?"

The woman looks startled for a moment, then draws

herself up proudly. "I've been doing both since I was a mere babe."

"Then you'll sit at your mistress's side and entertain her. Keep her mind off the pain."

Eneko puts a hand over his heart as the woman moves away, then bows to me.

"And you think you're not qualified to call yourself a physician?" He shakes his head in disbelief. "For the love of all the saints, set fire to that thought once and for all."

I smile a little. "You've not seen me do anything but order folk around. That's not being a physician."

"They listen to you, don't they?" he points out. "Getting people to follow your commands isn't easy. I know. It's the hardest part of captaining a ship."

When the guards return, they've got everything but the poppy milk. Instead, they've gotten a vial of jusquiam.

"But I asked for poppy milk." I frown, weighing the vial in my hand.

One of the guards shrugs, unperturbed. "This is what the apothecary gave us. He knows best."

I'd planned to visit an apothecary myself tomorrow, so I'll fetch poppy milk then. For now, I administer an herbal elixir with a measure of ground willow bark to ease the pain, then Signora Tarrag drinks her infusion of nettles without complaint. Her pain eases, and soon she's propped against silk-covered cushions, sipping chamomile and catswort tea while the old woman tells her some tale.

I can almost hear Uncle Dante's voice approving my choice of remedies, can practically see his loving smile. I straighten my shoulders as resolve flows through me.

Whatever it takes, however I can manage it, I *will* be a physician. This is what I was born to do. Uncle Dante often told me so. And until the day of his death, I believed it.

Despite everything, despite my uncertain future, I will not abandon my dream now.

Signora Tarrag beckons to me, and I lean close to hear her murmured words. "I saw you whispering with Captain Eneko at the door. Is he your lover, the Basque?"

I say nothing in response. Her lips curve in a languid smile, and her eyes are heavy-lidded. My silence doesn't seem to bother her; the herbal remedies are fogging her senses.

"He'll slip through your fingers like seawater," she slurs. "I warn you, signorina. He'll keep you hoping, string you along with promises, and then vanish when it suits him."

CHAPTER 16

I ASK a servant to take me to Signora Tarrag's chamber shortly after dawn. She is sleeping soundly, and her forehead is cool. But her pain will return, and it will only get worse as the tumor grows.

Back in my chamber, I'm relieved to see Rosetta's arm wound is looking better. The rash on her face has completely vanished.

My clothing was taken to the laundress during supper last night. I feel a bit foolish wearing silk, but my black wool cloak conceals the red dress from curious eyes as Signora Tarrag's guards lead Rosetta and I through the streets of Mdina. I admire the fine homes we pass, with carved stone lintels over the doorways, clever niches holding pots of orange-and-pink flowers, and ornate ironwork on the heavy wooden doors.

The guards lead us to an apothecary shop near the high walls of the city. At the end of the lane, I spy a group of humbly dressed people moving in our direction. Several more figures emerge from the shadows just beyond them.

I turn to the guards. "Where are those people coming from?"

"The Greek Gate," the larger man replies. "It's reserved for servants and slaves."

We enter the shop. Rows of wooden cabinets line the walls, the more valuable items stored behind a counter of cypress wood. The apothecary greets the guards with familiarity, then looks at me with wary curiosity.

"I visit on behalf of Signora Tarrag," I say. "I had asked for pure poppy milk last night. A vial of jusquiam was given to the guards instead."

"I've not seen you in Mdina before, signorina." He taps one finger on the counter in a quick rhythm, studying me with shrewd dark eyes.

"I've come with a friend of Signor Tarrag's. I'm trained in the art of healing."

He gives me a sharp look. "What do you mean by that?"

"I studied at the Schola Medica in Salerno."

The apothecary's eyebrows lift in surprise. "They still admit women?"

"Of course. Women have been both students and professors at the school since the days of Trotula de Ruggiero, the most skilled physician of Salerno."

He does not need to know I was the only woman in my class. Trotula de Ruggiero would be saddened to see what her beloved Schola Medica has become.

"Female physician, you mean to say," he replies in a haughty tone.

Ignoring his comment, I study the Venetian glass jars lined up on shelves behind him.

"Regarding the poppy milk, signor, do you have it?"

He sighs. "My supply is limited."

"Still, Signora Tarrag wants it, and I'm sure you don't want to displease her."

He squints at me. "Jusquiam will do the trick. I assure you, the Tarrag household is accustomed to the remedy."

"That may be, but when it's prepared by someone other than myself, I can't gauge which parts of the plant have been used. The leaves can kill—I've seen it happen more than once."

"My potion contains no leaves. Only seeds." The apothecary makes a harrumphing sound in the back of his throat. "I see you have indeed been well trained. Perhaps Salerno has not lost its way, after all."

"What do you speak of, signor?"

He leans both elbows on the counter. "I heard the school had fallen on hard times after the plague and never recovered. Some of the professors aren't even paid a salary. They keep teaching out of the kindness of their hearts, I suppose. But kindness doesn't put food on the table."

Rosetta pulls on my sleeve. "By all the saints, your uncle was probably one of them that didn't take money for his trouble. Such a good-hearted—"

I silence her with a look, my mind roiling with thoughts of Uncle Dante. Rosetta is right. If anyone had volunteered to go without a salary, I'm certain it would have been him. That would explain his debt to Signor Lucchesi. How could my uncle have known the wool merchant's generosity would abruptly end with his death?

"The poppy milk, signor?" I repeat.

Reluctantly, he selects a green glass vial from the shelf behind him. "Use it sparingly," he says. "My supplier vanished this winter, and I've yet to find a new one."

After purchasing a few other items for my personal supply of healing remedies, I wish the man good day and lead Rosetta to the door. As my eyes adjust to the brighter light outside, I bend my head to hers.

"From now on, do not speak of our past. Not a word to anyone! Do you understand?"

She sighs in aggravation. "What am I to talk of, then?"

"The weather. Food. Birdsong. There's plenty to speak about without sharing information that could get us in trouble."

I set off down the alley with the other three in my wake. When we enter the courtyard of the Tarrag residence, Eneko is pacing over the cobblestones. His tense expression lightens when our eyes meet.

"Giuliana! I was ready to come after you." He lowers his voice. "Signor Tarrag has inspected the falcons and given me leave to go. We'll depart this afternoon."

"Gladly." I glance toward the doorway leading inside. "I must attend to Signora Tarrag first."

A strange look passes over his face, but he stays silent.

Rosetta crosses her arms over her chest. "Am I permitted to tell you I'm hungry?"

"Yes," I say. "Harvest more nettle leaves from the garden for me, then go to the kitchens. Remember, weather, birds . . ."

"You don't have to remind me!" She stalks off, scowling.

"Cheeky servant you have," Eneko observes.

"She never learned to be discreet, but she's loyal and a good cook. She loved my uncle nearly as much as I did."

"And you love her."

His words are delivered so softly I strain to hear them.

"I need to . . . protect her, I suppose. She's taken care of me for a long time."

His lips quirk in a half-smile. "There are a few people who've found places in my heart, too. Keeping them safe is always at the top of my mind."

I nod slowly, wondering who those people are. Signora Tarrag's words last night rise up in my mind. Did she and

Eneko have some sort of romantic attachment gone awry? Part of me wants to inquire about it, but the courtyard is full of servants, and it would be foolish to gossip about their mistress in this public space.

When I'm admitted to Signora Tarrag's chambers, she is sitting at a table by the windows, applying kohl to her eyelids. Her attendants bustle around, laying out garments and jewelry. The color has returned to her face; she looks well rested.

I'm relieved at the sight, grateful that my decisions last night were sound. It strikes me that if she had worsened during the night, I would likely have been blamed. I swallow hard, keeping my expression stone-still.

"Ah, there you are." Signora Tarrag completes her task and stands. "Your elixirs and teas are just what I needed. I can't believe I've gone this long without them."

Her lips stretch in a wide smile, but her eyes show something else. A cool, calculating assessment.

"Signora, you flatter me. Here—" I place the vial of poppy milk on her table. "Just a scant spoonful before bedtime, no more. It will help you sleep and take care of any pain. The apothecary does not have a reliable supplier any longer, it seems. It would be wise to find another supply soon, for you'll need it."

She nods. "My husband will make sure we never want for poppy milk again."

She dismisses her other attendants. I watch them file out the doorway, and a prickle of foreboding crawls up my spine.

Signora Tarrag picks up the poppy milk and twirls the vial in her fingertips. "You should have finished your studies. Your training is too valuable to waste. I wish to reward you, signorina, by making you my personal physician."

All the air leaves my lungs. "Would your husband approve?" I ask in astonishment.

"My husband's approval is secondary."

I must look skeptical because her eyes narrow and she puts the vial down with a thump.

"My first husband was much older than me. He beat me often, but I gave him many sons, and I was as sweet as honey to him. When he died, I was a wealthy woman." A faraway look comes over her face. "He left me gold and properties— including land by the coast and fertile grain fields—and he commanded our sons to keep building our fortune at sea. I married Signor Tarrag because my sons wanted the alliance. With his fleet at their disposal, my sons now command a vast network of ships throughout the Mediterranean. Do you see now, signorina? I am a woman of power. If I say you are a physician, everyone on this island will accept it as a fact."

Stunned, I can produce no words of response. I manage a slow nod.

"We would protect you as if you were our own kin, were you to live with us," she goes on. "Your servant remarked upon your love for your aunt in Genoa and of your devotion to women of the lower classes. Your aunt would be welcome to visit as often as she pleases. And I'll send you into our community to heal others. It would be my honor."

I hesitate. Could I fulfill my life's ambition here in Mdina? Could I achieve the future I thought I'd lost forever?

"We'll pay you handsomely," Signora Tarrag goes on, holding my gaze. "You'll have a suite of chambers in our home. Your servant will be your lady's maid, treated with respect. I see how you adore her."

I stiffen as she casts her net of spider's silk over me, spinning a gilded future that is as fragile as a puff of smoke. If one more person uses Rosetta as chattel to get me to do what they want—

"Thank you, signora. But I cannot stay here." The words tumble out in a rush. "My aunt is expecting me in Genoa. I have a future there."

She closes the space between us. "Do you? There is a certain Florentine merchant who would argue that your future is in Florence, by his side. As his wife. Your servant told anyone who would listen that you broke a contract of marriage when you left Salerno. I very much doubt your betrothed has forgotten. And my husband can easily communicate your whereabouts to the man."

How quickly powerful people turn to coercion when they don't get their way.

"I am sure he already knows I'm headed to Genoa. I don't care if he learns where I am."

Even as I speak, my knees begin trembling. I recall Signor Lucchesi's florid face, his anger at my defiance, and fear grips my throat.

She pounces. "You would be safe from him here. I vow it."

And then I look into her fathomless eyes and I know only one thing with certainty: this place is not safe for me or for Rosetta. We must leave with Eneko, no matter what awaits us on his ship in those wild, shifting seas.

"You are so kind, so generous to think of me for this role," I say in a measured voice. "But I cannot accept. Thank you for your hospitality, signora. I shall never forget it."

I wheel and stride away. Her simmering fury pursues me all the way down the corridor. As soon as I turn the corner, I break into a run.

CHAPTER 17

WE COLLECT our things in haste. After a frustrating exchange with a servant who tells me my clothes are being laundered elsewhere and need more time to dry, I resign myself to wearing red silk for the duration of my journey. We follow Eneko to the courtyard, where the strike of hooves on stone mingles with the soft gurgle of water in the fountain.

"Here." He hands me up onto the wagon bench, and I slip my satchel's strap over my shoulder. "Signor Tarrag was none too pleased to learn you'd refused his wife's offer. He won't be seeing us off."

I look at him in alarm. "Are we in danger because of what I did?"

"Danger is everywhere, all the time."

His answer does not reassure me. As he mounts his horse, a pair of servants push open the great wooden doors. The driver slaps the mules with his reins, and the wheels creak into motion.

We enter the street, and Eneko's mounted men—who have been staying in a nearby inn—fall in around us, swords strapped at their hips.

We cross the broad square Rosetta and I had passed through on our way to the apothecary. A few vendors lead donkeys into the square from various small lanes, the animals' packs bursting with goods. Their talk is about tomorrow's market. In the morning, this square will bustle with merchants and traders hawking their goods to Mdina's prosperous citizens.

As we move toward the city gates, my thoughts turn to the letter from Aunt Amalia hidden in my bodice, next to my heart. Proof of our connection. Proof that my plan to throw myself on my aunt's mercy isn't madness—

A sudden movement to my left breaks my reverie. Three men dart out from the gloom of an alleyway, running straight for the cart. Instinctively, I throw an arm around Rosetta, who shrinks into me like a child.

Then rough hands clutch at me, and I'm yanked from the mule cart in one savage motion. I scream, writhing and fighting to get free.

One man clutches me to him. He's huge, and I recognize him as Signora Tarrag's guard. He drags me toward the alley, flanked by his companions.

"Giuliana!" Eneko's voice slices through the melee.

I wind my legs around my captor's feet, attempting to trip him. He repels me like a dog shaking off a puppy, tightening his grip on my arms. One of the other men seizes me by the feet, and the pair of them lift me airborne. My satchel falls on the ground with a thud.

A flash of black looms in my line of sight, then two more. Eneko and his men lunge at my captors, swords flashing, and I'm dumped on the unforgiving cobbles. Rolling away from the men, I grab my satchel, spring up, and run for the cart.

"Move!" I scream at Rosetta, tugging her off the wagon bench.

"They'll follow us!" she moans. "They'll catch us!"

I don't dare make for the main gate. What if more attackers lurk there, waiting to snatch us? Instead, I lead Rosetta to the lane where we'd seen the Greek Gate on our outing to the apothecary.

The gate is open, admitting a stream of servants and slaves, some carrying baskets, others riding in donkey carts.

I slow to a walk and have Rosetta follow behind me. We ease into the crowd, threading our way around people, animals, and carts. Together, we exit the city walls.

Rows of cypress trees extend along either side of the roadway, casting long shadows on the dusty ground. A crow rasps at us from a hidden perch with harsh, relentless cries.

"Put your hood on and bow your head," I tell Rosetta. "We'll make for the sea—"

Pounding hooves drown out my words. Eneko and his men ride from the main gates and bear down on us, the horses wild-eyed, the men bent low over their mounts' necks.

Eneko draws abreast of me. "Ride with me!" he orders. I take his outstretched hand, scramble up behind him, and clasp my arms around his waist.

One of his men rides close to Rosetta and snatches her up, settling her on the saddle before him. She lets out an indignant squawk of protest, but when she realizes it's Beñat, she calms quickly.

We canter off, pounding down the main road away from Mdina in tight formation. I pray no one is following us. If Signor Tarrag wished it, he could have us surrounded and disarmed in minutes.

The morning sun blazes overhead in a brilliant, cloudless sky. At a fork in the road, we veer to a smaller track that I don't recall from our journey to Mdina. We are not returning to the harbor where Eneko's ship is anchored, I realize with dismay.

"Where are we going?" I call out over the thundering hooves.

Eneko doesn't answer. I burrow into his back, breathing in his mingled scents of leather, sun-warmed flax cloth, sweat, and something bright and sharp—perhaps rosemary oil. Under my cheek, his muscles tense and relax in rhythm with the horse's motion. Though I'm afraid, I also feel exhilarated by the warmth of his body and his confident handling of the horse. I tighten my arms around him, thanking God for his presence.

We ride past a settlement of farmhouses and a patchwork of fields. Then a rise in the road takes us high enough that I spy the shimmering turquoise waters of a half-moon-shaped bay. The dark outline of a ship looms far from shore.

"That's where we're going." Eneko says. "Gnejna Bay. Otherwise known as Pirate's Cove."

A grippo waits for us in the curving embrace of a rocky inlet, bobbing in the swells.

Dismounting on the beach, I shade my brow with a hand and study the landscape. There are no other ships in the bay. Behind us, the hills rise sharply, blocking our view of the road. A lone tower sits on a stone outcropping that juts into the water. Its arrow slits gape at us like dark unblinking eyes.

"Why weren't we followed?" I ask Eneko, who is over-seeing his men as they gather their belongings from the saddlebags. "Signor Tarrag rules these lands."

"I'm too valuable to him," he says. "Especially now."

"Why is that?"

"Thanks to your advice, his wife needs a steady supply of poppy milk. This year, my tribute to him was falcons. Next year, it's to be poppy milk."

"Is that an improvement over falcons?"

"If I can get my hands on a good supply of poppy milk, it will be."

He unsaddles his mount, removes its bit and bridle, and gives it a slap on the rump. It trots away in the direction we came, tail flicking.

One by one, the other men follow suit. The horses amble away, never looking back.

In the shallows, Eneko sweeps me into his arms and settles me in the boat.

I look him in the eyes and ask the question that's been burning in my mind. "What is between you and Signora Tarrag?"

"Beñat!" he calls out, ignoring my question. "Carry Signorina Rosetta."

Beñat scoops her up and places her next to me, grinning. Rosetta preens at his attention, returning the smile.

The men begin rowing. I huddle on the rough plank next to Rosetta, my satchel tucked against my chest.

Eneko lets out a curse, then says something in a fierce, urgent tone to the rowers. They increase their pace, dipping the oars into the water and pulling them out again, chanting something in Basque all the while. I whip my head around to see what sparked his words. A row of horsemen lines the shore, roaring obscenities. Another group of horses surrounds the tower looming above us, and soon I hear shouting from within it. My stomach clenches as a volley of arrows flies our way.

The arrows slice through the air nearby and vanish into the water. The rowers never break their rhythm.

Rosetta begins to weep. "Saints in heaven, we'll be murdered!"

"But Signor Tarrag thinks you're too valuable to kill!" I shout at Eneko.

"Agreed." Eneko pulls crude wooden shields from under the benches and distributes them to the men, who brace them against the boat's hull like a makeshift wall. "His wife is another matter. That's her tower, and those are her men."

"Is her vengeance directed at me or at you?" I demand.

"We've both denied her what she wants. We're both her targets now."

I clutch Rosetta to me. "We're nearly to the ship," I tell her.

This isn't exactly true. The ship looks like a toy from this distance.

More arrows arc past, closer this time. I shut my eyes. Rosetta prays aloud, naming saint after saint, pleading to Santa Maria above all to protect us.

Arrows hammer into the boat's wooden hull with sickening thuds.

Then one of the rowers cries out in pain and slumps over his oar.

Rosetta screams. I cover her mouth with a hand. The last thing these men need is a distraction.

Eneko leaps to his crewman's aid, deftly positioning him near the bow. He gives me a pleading glance. I nod, understanding at once, and turn to Rosetta.

"Keep your head down, be quiet as a rabbit, and keep saying your prayers."

With that, I crawl to the injured man's side.

An arrow juts from his right shoulder. Blood stains his shirt around the shaft. It will have to be removed, the wound cauterized. For now, all I can do is stabilize his body as best I can and offer him words of comfort. I remove my cloak and wad it up, then gently slide it under his head. His skin is a terrible shade of gray.

Beñat bellows suddenly. I look up to see blood gushing from a wound on his scalp. An arrow must have skimmed his head, tearing flesh as it went.

"Give him your shirt and tell him to press it hard against

the wound to staunch the blood," I tell the closest crewman. "Make him lie down."

He quickly obeys.

Eneko, seated in a wounded rower's place, powers his oar through the water with an expression of grim ferocity. We've nearly reached the ship. The arrows no longer hit their marks, but drop harmlessly into the swells.

For the moment, it seems, we are safe.

CHAPTER 18

"Anchors up!" Eneko shouts when we're safely aboard his galley. "See to the wounded, Giuliana," he adds over his shoulder. "Take them to my cabin."

I instruct several men to carry the severely injured oarsman, then follow with Rosetta, whose arm is twined around Beñat.

"He saved me from the bad men of Mdina," she says with a defensive edge in her voice. "Least I can do is return the favor."

The men lead the way to Eneko's cabin in the stern near the kitchen. The cramped space is filled with a built-in bed, a desk and stool, and several wooden cabinets attached to the walls.

"Put both men on the bed. The arrow must face up, though. Here." I place my folded-up cloak on the head of the bed. "He can rest his cheek on that."

Beñat balks. "Fine for him, but I don't need to lie down. I need a bandage, that's all."

"You'll lie abed until I clean and staunch the wound," I

tell him. "Otherwise, you'll keep bleeding. Scalps love to bleed."

Beñat, admonished by my stern tone, falls into silence. Carefully, the men lay their comrades on the bed.

One man asks uncertainly, "Should we remove their boots?"

Rosetta snorts. "Blessed be, certainly not! This room smells bad enough as it is."

I turn to the able-bodied men ranged around us. "Fetch us hot water, linens, wine, and . . . Do you have any herbs, ointments, medicines on this ship?"

"They'd be in the captain's cabinets, signorina," Beñat says cheerfully, pressing his hand to his bleeding head. "But himself's got the key."

"One of you fetch the captain, then," I order to the others. "The rest of you, get the supplies I mentioned. Please hurry!"

The men crowd through the door.

As soon as a sailor bounds back into the cabin with wine, hot water, and linens, I feel better.

"I'll have to sew up the head wound. Fetch the kit from my satchel, Rosetta."

I give Beñat a few gulps from the wine jug.

"Do you need to wait for the wine to take effect, Signor Beñat, or can I stitch you now?"

He gives an indifferent shrug. "Do what you must."

I soak a square of linen in wine and clean the wound as best I can. Beñat endures my ministrations in silence, his eyes fixed on the floor.

"Cheer up," Rosetta advises him, offering wine to the other injured man. "The signorina knows what she's doing."

"Oh, I'm happy. Can't muster a smile at the moment, that's all," he says through gritted teeth.

I prepare Uncle Dante's fine steel needle with a length of silk thread, then make quick work of the sutures.

"There." I tie off the ends of the thread, step back, and nod. "You'll do."

Beñat slowly sits up. "By all the saints, that stings."

"I can give you a tea with willow bark," I tell him. "As soon as we take care of your friend."

Eneko appears through the doorway. "What do you need, Signorina Giuliana?"

"Poppy milk. Butterwort ointment. Honey. Chamomile. And someone to make tea with this." I fumble in my satchel for the small supply of willow bark powder I purchased from the apothecary in Mdina.

Eneko jangles a keyring at his waist, unlocking a cabinet. "Poppy milk I have. As for the rest . . . well, I've got honey. And plenty more wine. It'll help with that one." He gestured at the badly wounded man.

"Coming through with fire!" a voice yells, and a man with a red-tipped poker walks gingerly into the cabin. "Is this what you wanted, signorina?"

I regard the glowing stick of iron. "Yes. Hold it aloft for now."

Eneko holds out a smooth bit of wood. "Oak from Basque country."

I slip it between the man's teeth and instruct him to bite down.

Studying the broken arrow tip jutting from his shoulder, I hesitate for a moment. Then, exchanging a quick glance with Eneko, I murmur, "You've done this before, I'm guessing."

He nods.

"Will you pull the arrow out? Then I'll cauterize it."

He steps in front of me, so close I feel the sinewy outlines of his lean, muscled back pressing against my breasts.

I draw in a long breath, absorbing his scent, taking strength from him.

"Now," I say.

With one swift motion, he pulls up on the arrow shaft and tears it free. The man groans in agony as his wound oozes blood. I douse it in wine, then hand the jug to Eneko and take hold of the poker.

With steady determination, I press the red-hot tip of the poker into the wound. The sizzle and stink of burned flesh fills the air. My stomach turns. I try not to hear the agonized groans of the wounded man, focusing all my concentration on assuring the wound is fully cauterized.

Moaning, the man grinds his head into the mattress.

"You'll live," Eneko mutters, leaning close to his sailor. "It'll hurt for a while, but you'll live. Thank the sun and stars. I wouldn't want to be the one to tell your wife you'd died."

CHAPTER 19

For days, I tend to the man's wound, cleaning and dressing it with care. It does not fester, thanks to the nettles I've brought from Mdina. Uncle Dante would be proud, I think as I smear ointment on the sailor's shoulder one afternoon. He sits on a stool at Eneko's desk, and for the first time his posture is straight. His color is good, his eyes bright.

Rosetta bursts through the door carrying a bowl of something hot and fragrant. "Captain told me to bring this to him." She advances, wielding a wooden spoon in her other hand. "Shall I feed you, sir?"

He shakes his head. "I can do it."

"Suit yourself." Rosetta plunks the bowl and spoon on the desk. "The men are asking about you. They crowd me in the kitchen, bothering me with their questions. Especially Beñat."

The man brightens. "How's his head?"

"Healing nicely, thanks to the signorina."

The ship lurches suddenly. Rosetta lunges forward and cradles the bowl with both hands, but soup has already sloshed over the rim.

"Better eat it quick," she advises. "There's a storm coming from the north—that's what the captain told me. He's making everyone eat now so the food goes in their bellies and not on the deck."

Unease grips my chest. I sink down on the stool at Eneko's desk, securing the buckles on my satchel. In a storm, things scatter. Whatever happens, I have to keep track of my possessions.

The injured man slurps the soup in loud gulps, not bothering with the spoon. Then he wipes his mouth with his sleeve.

"I'm well enough to attend to my duties. In a storm, all hands on deck. That's the law of the sea." He smooths a hand over his beard. "Excepting you, signorinas. You'll stay out of harm's way, safe in the captain's cabin."

"We can go back to our own cabin." I stand.

Then the ship plows into a massive wave, its timbers creaking. The floor seems to drop beneath me. I nearly fall, but Rosetta reaches out and steadies me.

The Basque puts a hand over his heart and bows slightly. "I'll always be grateful to you for saving my life. *Eskerrik asko.* Thank you."

As he leaves, I notice Rosetta's face is an unnatural shade of gray-green.

"Go to our cabin and lie down," I say.

"But this mess . . ." Her voice is thin and weak.

"I'll be fine. Hurry, before the swells get worse."

Reluctantly, she trundles off.

I regard the bloodstained linens on the bed, wondering if pirate ships carry extra bedclothes.

For some reason, the absurd thought sparks a laugh that sweeps through me like a gust of bracing wind. Soon I'm doubled over, shoulders shaking, marveling at the predicament I've found myself in.

Footsteps sound behind me. "Signorina! Are you ill? Hurt?"

I straighten and turn to face Eneko, still smiling, and shake my head.

He studies me, eyes brightening. Reaching out, he lays a gentle hand along my cheek. A current of attraction ripples between us, and I lean into his touch.

"You have blood on your face," he says softly. "Let me wipe it off."

I stand very still, heart pounding, as he wets a length of linen from a jug of water, then rubs it on my skin.

Just as it had before, his skin against mine ignites something warm and thrilling in my veins. I forget the storm, the injured men, the flight from Mdina, my uncertain future . . . Everything falls away as I close my eyes and allow myself to savor the moment.

Without meaning to, I let out a sigh.

He stops. "What's wrong?"

"Nothing." My eyelids lids flutter open. "Every muscle in my body has been wound tight as thread on a spool since we left Signor Tarrag's house. This is the first time I've relaxed enough to take a deep breath."

He nods, understanding. The ship lurches, sending our bodies on a collision course. Entangled, attempting to regain our footing, we both laugh.

I tilt my head back, savoring the joyful light in Eneko's eyes.

And then his lips touch mine. A blast of pleasure courses through me, sending a path of fire from my heart through every vein in my body. I kiss him eagerly in return. His kiss becomes deeper, his warm lips more insistent.

I embrace him, tracing the contours of his back and shoulders with my fingers, and pull him closer.

He follows the outline of my jaw with his mouth, then

finds the pulse point on my neck and nuzzles it until my knees buckle. I let out a moan of pleasure, fitting the length of my body to his.

"Eneko," I whisper. "Eneko."

Then the urgent shouts of men on deck shatter our idyll.

He steps back, his expression guilty.

"Signorina, I should not have done that. I apologize. Let me accompany you to your cabin."

I take his hand and place it over my heart. "Don't apologize. I liked it."

His worried look fades. "Truly?"

"Why do you doubt my words? I speak the truth."

"I've noticed that," he says drily. "You do speak your mind."

"Captain!" a man cries from above decks. "We need you!"

Eneko raises my hand to his lips. "I can't neglect my duties any longer."

"Go. I'm safe here. No need to worry about me."

"That's where you're wrong," he murmurs, leaning close again. "All I've done since we met is worry about you, Giuliana."

The storm-lashed ship bucks and heaves most of the night. Next to me, Rosetta moans and mumbles prayers, curled tight like a nut in a shell.

But the gale eases just before dawn. Rosetta falls into a deep sleep punctuated by fitful snoring. For my part, I've never felt so exhilarated. My skin tingles, still charged with desire from my encounter with Eneko. I imagine our kisses and caresses over and over, mesmerized by the shiver of longing that courses through me each time.

Without making the conscious decision, without making

a sound, I rise from the bed and slip out the door. Wading through the darkness one silent step at a time, I stop in front of Eneko's cabin. My heart pounds against my ribs so wildly I press a hand over my breastbone in a futile attempt to calm it.

What am I doing? What am I setting in motion?

Since I was a young girl, I've been resolved not to marry. But have I ever vowed not to take a lover?

No.

Even as I have the thoughts, I raise a hand to knock.

Before I make a sound, the door opens. Eneko stands there, an oil lamp in one hand, his sword in the other.

"By the sun and stars, woman, what are you doing here? I might have hurt you!" His voice is harsh, and a flush of chagrin sweeps over me.

"Forgive me. I wanted to—" I falter, not sure what to say next.

What *do* I want? I want to be close to him. To touch his warm skin, to hear his heart pounding in his chest, to feel his taut, sinewy muscles under my fingertips.

As if a current of water has pushed me from behind, I close the space between us and kiss him.

He steps back, eyes widening. "Are you sure?" he asks softly, placing the sword and the oil lamp on the desk.

I nod. "I am."

He shuts the door and latches it, then turns to me with an expression of such tenderness and delight that my heart swells with joy.

Without speaking, he pulls me into his arms, both hands cupping my face. He kisses me with a reverence that elates me, mapping a path along my cheekbones, my forehead, my jawline, and then seeks my lips with his warm, strong mouth. My skin is exquisitely sensitive under his touch, tingling and sparking with desire.

I exult in the taste of him, kissing him back with a hunger that surprises me. I sweep my hands along the hard muscles of his arms and the solid planes of his chest, then rest my palms on his firm, curving backside. He lets out a quiet moan of pleasure.

"Can I take you to bed?" His voice is hoarse. "I'll be careful. I won't get you with child. I promise."

"There's nothing I would rather do on this ship, in this moment, than share your bed."

He sweeps me up in his arms and ceremoniously deposits me on the bed.

I smooth the fresh linens with a hand. "So you do have more than one set of sheets."

He grins. "We may be pirates, but we're not animals."

He strips off his nightshirt with one graceful motion. I take in the sight of his naked body with a sigh of appreciation. His lean body, sculpted with muscles hewn over decades, speaks of an active life at sea, and his skin is the light brown of new-cut oak.

Strangely, I don't feel a moment's hesitation about shedding my clothes in front of Eneko. Instead, I'm eager to disrobe in front of him, happy to see him smile in appreciation at the sight of me naked in his bed. And even happier when he slides onto the sheets, his body warm against mine.

"I feel safe with you," I whisper into his neck, luxuriating in his smooth skin. "Somehow I always have."

The pleasure that his touch ignites in me makes me gasp aloud. He's gentle, but there is no hesitance about his movements. He seems to know exactly how to please me.

He plants a kiss over my heart and meets my gaze.

"The day we met in the Salerno harbor, I recognized in you the same spirit that lives within me." He rests his cheek on my breast, speaking quietly, one hand spanning my stomach from hipbone to hipbone. "We were meant to find each other, Giuliana. Our whole lives were a journey taking us to that day."

A pulsing knot of desire and longing radiates through my core, warming me from within. Every muscle in my body seems coiled with delicious tension, and I long to surrender to it fully.

"I've learned so much about the human body, but I never knew until this moment how much pleasure we are capable of," I say in wonder. "Our bodies are miraculous."

Eneko raises his head and gives me a quizzical look. "Do I have a physician in my bed or a lover?"

I smile, twining my fingers through his dark hair and abandoning myself to his caresses, entering a dreamy state of rapture that I hope never ends.

"Both, Captain."

CHAPTER 20

THE PORT of Genoa shimmers on the horizon. Afternoon sunlight glints off the wooden masts of ships and the tile-roofed warehouses abutting the harbor. It seems impossible that we're already here, and yet the fortnight-long journey from Malta is over. Though I've longed to speed our voyage many times, I feel no jubilation at our arrival. Instead, I'm conflicted. At this moment, what I want is Eneko. The idea of leaving him makes my heart unbearably heavy.

I fill my lungs, tipping my face toward the sun. The swells are modest this afternoon, capped with swirls of foam, and I whisper a prayer of thanks to Santa Maria for our safe passage.

Even as I acknowledge my gratitude, worry descends on me like a sodden cloak. What lies ahead? Will I be able to practice medicine here? Will I be able to earn my own way through life, or will I be forced to marry in the end?

Don't think about tomorrow, I order myself. Think only of today.

"Ready?" Eneko's voice cuts through my thoughts.

I turn to him, unable to hide the sorrow welling up in me at our impending separation. Every night since our first clandestine encounter in his quarters, I've crept into his bed and surrendered to a feverish longing for him that has taken command of me, body and soul. I can still taste his kisses on my lips, feel them burning paths of pleasure over my skin. Looking into his eyes, I know he feels the same way. If I could embrace him here, now, before his entire crew, I would do it in a heartbeat.

But instead, I stay where I am. I muster a calm tone and say, "I'm ready to be off these wild seas."

"And what about your new life in Genoa?"

I study the distant port. It's crowded with ships, their masts slicing into the sky like swords. "I'm hopeful."

He leans his forearms on the gunwale. "I've never seen this harbor so packed with vessels. Some event is happening in Genoa. Springtime is full of feast days—so many saints to honor." He looks at me, his voice softening. "You can change your mind. Stay aboard. You could be the physician we've always needed but never found. See what magic you've wrought?" He glances at Beñat, who is laughing at something Rosetta said near the kitchen in the stern. "His head is fully healed. And my gunner's shoulder will make a full recovery thanks to you, pirate's physician."

"If we could distill the world down to you and me, I'd make your ship my home, Eneko. Pirate's physician, though? I don't merit the title, I'm afraid."

He stands tall, spreading both arms wide. "Consider this voyage your medical examination. I now deem you a practicing physician."

I smile, reveling in the merriment that crackles in his golden-brown eyes, then succumb to the doubt that has nagged at me since Malta. "I've asked you many times, and now this is the last," I say. "What was between you and Signora Tarrag?"

His expression sobers. "The less time talking about her, the better."

"Make it quick, then."

"When I first met her, she was a widow interested in taking a lover." He's avoiding my gaze now.

"And did you return her interest?"

"A rich widow is free to do as she wishes. As is a man. Two people, free to do as they wish, often act upon their desires . . ."

"You've got a way with words, Captain," I say tartly. "If you get tired of piracy, you could always turn to the law."

"I'll remember that," he says, grinning. Then his face darkens. "Whatever passed between myself and Signora Tarrag meant nothing. There's never been a woman like you on my ship—"

"Or in your bed?" I cut in, still smarting at the idea of his dalliance with Signora Tarrag. "How many have there been? How many more will there be?"

He stares at me in complete seriousness. "There have been many. I won't lie. But none who are your equal. You are my love, Giuliana. My heart. Sail with us. Come east as our physician, mending the illnesses and injuries of my crew. You'd see extraordinary places. Rhodes first, then Cyprus, Alexandria, Damascus. The Holy Land."

"And I'd share your bed," I add in a teasing lilt, the sting already gone from my discovery. "You left out that part."

He twines his fingers around mine, and I draw in a breath at the charge of pleasure his touch ignites.

"I've never known what it is to truly love a man, nor to share his bed," I confess. "The truth is now that I've tasted life with you, the thought of anything else is bleak."

He moves to embrace me, his eyes bright with tears. I watch him fight the impulse, and he stills himself, his face twisting with regret. Our hands still link us, though, and he strokes my palm with his thumb. My body hums with desire. If I could only capture this sensation and carry it—him—with me always.

I take in a long breath, trying to compose my thoughts. "I've imagined a future together many times during this voyage. But your ship is a man's world, Eneko. As are the seas. What if your galley is captured? What would become of me? I'd likely be taken captive, sold into slavery at some distant port." I shake my head. "You know it as well as I do."

"It's hard to accept the idea of never seeing you again, that's all." His voice drops. "I can't marry, Giuliana. I sail the seas for years at a time. I won't leave a wife behind, wondering if I'm alive or dead. That's no way to live."

"I've never wished to marry either," I reply. "I was raised to become a physician. That's still what I want."

"You have the strength and the skill to practice medicine," he says fiercely. "I believe you'll find a way to claim that future in this city, with your aunt's help."

I wish my confidence matched his. "Come back to Genoa, then," I say. "Make it a regular stop on your travels between Basqueland and the eastern seas."

"I'd like nothing more," he says. "It would ease the pain of parting, that's certain."

"Then plan on it." A wave of sorrow strikes me, but I push it away, smiling. "I'll walk to the harbor each month and look for your banners."

"Probably better than to have me appear at your aunt's doorstep. She lives in one of Genoa's finer quarters. Not a fitting neighborhood for a man like me." He grins wickedly. "When I return, I can rent chambers for us. You can come examine whatever ails me. I'm sure I'll have pent-up needs to attend to."

I widen my eyes, more delighted than shocked by his words. It's a lovely game, this dream of ours. If this is to be the pattern of my life, so be it. I decided long ago I'd never marry, and during this voyage with Eneko, I've made an equally bold decision: I will not live the virtuous life of a nun either.

"I'll attend to your needs if you attend to mine," I say. "I'll require a fluffy featherbed, silken pillows, a copper tub filled with steaming water and jasmine oil . . ."

The trumpeters drown out my words with a blast from their perch by the navigator, heralding the approach to Genoa. Below decks, the rowers push their oars into the water and sing a rhythmic chant. A crewman pipes a series of signals with his whistle, setting various sailors into motion all around the deck.

Eneko groans and slides his hand reluctantly from my grasp. "I want to kiss you. Not captain my ship."

"Your men would not appreciate that," I say. "Though in truth, I would."

Rummaging in his coin purse, he retrieves a handful of golden florins and presses them into my palm. When I protest, he shakes his head.

"Money means safety, Giuliana. Take it for your protection and Rosetta's."

I stare at the pile of coins in my hand, relenting. They'll go far to supplement Uncle Dante's savings and make me feel a bit more confident about the coming weeks and months. As I transfer the money to my own purse, Eneko runs a hand through his thick black hair and sighs.

"Don't forget me, Giuliana. You have no fear of me forgetting you."

A convoy of Genoese military vessels is anchored at the

perimeter of the harbor, just inside the stone seawalls that partially enclose the port. As we pass the ships, Eneko moves along the bow to return the greeting of a Genoese captain. They have a brief shouted exchange.

I draw closer. "What did he say?"

"The wool market begins soon." He gestures at the ships anchored in the harbor. "These are merchant ships from England, Flanders, France—and more are coming." His expression grows conflicted. "The captain asked us to join the Genoese convoys heading to the island of Rhodes tomorrow."

"The Genoese invite pirates into their ranks?" I find that difficult to believe.

"I've worked for them many times as a privateer-for-hire. They're allies of the Knights Hospitaller of Rhodes, and the knights always need more privateers to help their cause." He studies the military ships with narrowed eyes. "We'll have to resupply quickly and get back out to sea straightaway. But it's a rare opportunity. Traveling without support in the eastern Mediterranean is more and more dangerous."

"Of course," I say. "You should join them."

He hesitates. "I wanted to stay in Genoa long enough to make certain you were welcome here."

"There's no need. My aunt will take us in the moment she sees us." I try to ignore the doubt that has plagued me since we left Salerno. My aunt knows nothing of Uncle Dante's death, my journey, my thwarted betrothal.

"There will be Florentine merchants in the city for the wool market." Eneko's warning makes my muscles tighten, one by one.

What if Signor Lucchesi is here? I swallow, knowing I'll have to take that chance. What other choice do I have?

Eneko studies me thoughtfully, his jaw working. "Beñat lived in Genoa for a time as a younger man. He knows the city well. He and a few other Basques will accompany you and

Rosetta ashore. They'll serve as guards until you are sure of your situation."

"You'll leave Genoa without them?" I'm astonished.

"They'll do as I ask. Besides, they could use a respite from life at sea. Especially him." Eneko jerks his head at the man with the shoulder injury, who's doing his best to haul a coiled flax rope with one arm. "He's not fully mended yet."

"As you wish. But we don't need their help, truly. We'll have safe refuge here. I'm certain of it."

"I pray that it's so, Giuliana." His tone is grave. "Genoa is full of tricksters and thieves, like any port. You told me once you've used a dagger in your own defense. Are you ready to wield it once more?"

"Yes."

"When did you need it before?"

"A man's wife and son died the same day. Uncle Dante and I were in their home. In his grief, the man blamed Uncle Dante, said it was his potions, not the fever, that killed them. He snatched up his axe from the hearth and—" I stumble over the words, the terrible image still vivid in my mind. "He ran at Uncle Dante, waving the axe, cursing and shouting. I drew my blade and stabbed him from behind, in the shoulder. He dropped the axe, and the pain made his rage melt away."

Eneko gives me a look that conveys both pride and respect. "I'm glad to hear it. Until you're living under your aunt's roof, keep your dagger ready and trust no one."

I stay silent, longing to throw my arms around him. Grief rears up inside me, tearing at my heart. What if I never see him again? Will this be our last encounter?

No. No. No.

All I can do is repeat the word silently like an invocation, willing it to be true. We *will* meet again. I have no choice but to believe it. The alternative is crushing.

His face reflects the consternation I feel. But when the

trumpets blare, he clenches his jaw, rearranging his features into a composed and implacable expression, and strides off.

The details of his lean form blur as tears cloud my vision. I blink them away, watching him stop to talk with Beñat and Rosetta. Beñat throws a glance at me, nodding in response to something Eneko says.

Then Eneko moves on, dispensing orders as he goes.

CHAPTER 21

With Beñat and two other Basque sailors accompanying us, Rosetta and I join the queue at Genoa's city gates. When the guards demand a tariff for entry, I am grateful for my heavy purse.

We begin the long climb up the hill to Aunt Amalia's neighborhood. The streets teem with citizens returning from the fish market in the harbor. All around us, people shout greetings at one another, sometimes pausing mid-stride to exchange news and gossip with friends.

We trudge up a steep lane, following a group of servant women carrying wicker baskets full of fish. Their lively chatter centers on sailors and absent sweethearts. The topic makes me want to turn and catch one last glimpse of Eneko's three-masted ship.

Lulled into a dreamy state by our plodding pace, I imagine Eneko's departure tomorrow. I see him standing at the bow of his galley as it cuts through the waves, closing the distance to the pack of Genoese warships in the distance.

Santa Maria, keep him safe, I silently pray.

After a circuitous climb on the cobbled lanes, we emerge

into a square. Ahead of us a church looms, its bell tower jutting into the brilliant blue sky.

The group of women we'd followed vanishes into a lane near the church. Rosetta stops to catch her breath, an anxious tightness in her expression.

"Come, Rosetta." I take her arm. "We'll soon have fine lodging and a hot meal."

"In a strange city." Rosetta shakes off my hand. "I don't like Genoa. It smells of the sea, and there are too many hills."

"Salerno smells of the sea and has just as many hills," I retort.

Rosetta's frown deepens. "Yes, but it's home."

"Not far to the Piazza Caricamento," Beñat says with an encouraging smile. "Almost there, signorinas."

His knowledge of Genoa's streets is a comfort.

When we reach the piazza, I'm relieved to see a fine palazzo embellished with painted frescoes on the facade. It's just as my aunt had depicted in her long-ago letter; we are in the right place. Three guards wearing helmets, red leather armor, and formidable-looking swords stand in front of the structure.

Across from the palazzo, a more modest stone building is draped in mourning crepe. The black cloth flutters in the breeze. Rosetta crosses herself and casts a fearful glance skyward, as if Death still lingers, waiting to strike down his next victim.

I pull my aunt's letter from my bodice and unfurl it, studying the sketch she'd made of the square. I turn a slow circle, comparing the buildings I see to those in my aunt's drawing.

Reluctantly, I settle my gaze on the black-shrouded building. "That's it, over there."

Rosetta draws in a breath and raises her rosary beads to her lips. "Oh, God protect us. Your aunt is dead."

"By all the saints, don't say such things." I march forward, praying that Rosetta is wrong. The others follow closely behind.

At the door, I rap the bronze knocker. It's shaped like a dragon's head, and the metal is cool against my skin.

A manservant opens the door. "What is your business here?" he asks, looking us over with a frown. "This house is in mourning."

Straightening my shoulders, I summon a tone of authority. "I am Giuliana Rinaldi, niece of your mistress. I arrived by ship from Salerno today, and I wish to see my aunt Amalia. Please tell her I am here. I bring news of her brother, Dante Rinaldi."

The man looks surprised for a moment, but instead of welcoming us in, his brow furrows and he compresses his lips into a thin line. "My mistress is out. My master has died, and so she must attend to many things."

A current of relief floods my body. Thank God my aunt is still alive. "May God bless his soul. That is distressing news indeed. When is the funeral?" I ask.

"It was last week, signorina. At the church not a hundred paces from here." He gestures beyond the building I had taken for a palazzo. "My mistress goes there each day to pray for his soul's salvation."

The servant has not offered hospitality, and I'm not sure what to do.

"I did not have an opportunity to write and let Aunt Amalia know I was coming," I say hesitantly. "But my aunt has often invited me to stay with her here. May we come in?"

His gaze slips from me to Rosetta as he considers my request. There's something disconcerting in the way he studies us. Then he gives the Basque men a suspicious stare.

"The men have other lodging," I say. "But my servant and I need—" I almost say "refuge," then think better of it.

Before I can complete my sentence, the servant speaks again.

"During the period of mourning, no visitors are allowed. My mistress's orders were clear."

"I am not a visitor. I'm a member of Aunt Amalia's family."

He shrugs. "I'll tell my mistress you called, signorina . . . ?"

"Giuliana Rinaldi," I repeat. Under my cloak, I press a fingertip against Uncle Dante's ring, and the hard edge of it digs into my breastbone. "Please tell her I'll return tomorrow."

But the heavy oak door is already closing.

By the time Genoa's churches are tolling the next hour, Beñat has found us lodging in a respectable boardinghouse not far from my aunt's home. After paying the landlady to bring us supper and wine in our chamber, he and the other Basques depart for their own rented chambers closer to the harbor. He says they'll return tomorrow at noon and accompany us to Aunt Amalia's house again.

Our simple meal disappears in minutes, and by nightfall Rosetta is snoring under a rough homespun blanket, leaving me to fend off my worries alone in the dark. I wonder how Aunt Amalia is coping with the loss of her husband. When I first met my aunt, she was mourning the death of her first husband, a man she adored. This Genoese wool merchant was not much more than a stranger to her when she wed him, and she did not expect to find love in his arms.

My mind spins back more than a decade to the precious days I spent with my aunt as a ten-year-old girl in Salerno. After she was first widowed, she'd visited Salerno to take her mind off the sorrow. Aunt Amalia's first husband had been her true love, Uncle Dante often said. He was a notary and a skilled draftsman who took pleasure in drawing astrological charts. Aunt Amalia helped him by adding color to the charts with tempera paints, creating whimsical moons, suns, and stars with the tip of her fine sable brush. The creations supplemented the income they received from the notarial work and brought them a measure of wealth that would have contented them if they were only able to have children. After a half-dozen of these prosperous but childless years, Aunt Amalia's husband contracted a terrible fever and died.

Aunt Amalia was hollow-eyed and too thin when she arrived in Salerno, for grief had robbed her of an appetite. But she drew me into the circle of her arms every chance she got, smiling through her tears.

"She's always longed for a daughter," Uncle Dante explained when I asked him why my aunt cried and smiled all at once. "You make her heart glad, even though it's been broken."

The affection Aunt Amalia showered upon me was a revelation. Though Uncle Dante was a kind, patient man, he rarely embraced me. He showed his love in other ways, by teaching me the names of every bone in the human body, instructing me in reading, writing, and mathematics, and keeping me well clothed and fed.

When Aunt Amalia returned to Genoa several months later, she'd regained her curves thanks to Rosetta's cooking. And the faraway look in her eyes had faded. On the day of her departure, she told me she was ready for what lay ahead.

"And what lies ahead?" I asked.

"Another marriage, *cara* Giuliana."

"But you've just lost your husband! And you're so sad." The words seemed harsh, and I regretted them. "I mean to say—"

"I am sad," she said, "and I'm a widow. But I don't have enough money to stay a widow for long."

"But you can paint and draw! You'll sell your work as you've always done, won't you?"

Aunt Amalia shook her head. "Not without a man at my side. We got such work thanks to the notary business, and women cannot work as notaries. That life is over now. But there is good news. Your uncle got a letter last week from my late husband's eldest cousin, who lost his own wife not long ago. He already has children and doesn't long for more, but he wishes to marry again. He has asked for my hand in marriage, and my dear brother has given his blessing to the betrothal. If all goes well, I'll be the wife of a Genoese wool merchant soon."

"Do you love him?" I asked.

"Not at all. He's twice my age. In time, perhaps, I shall learn to love him."

I told her I didn't understand.

"You will one day. And if you stay true to your studies, you'll be a physician. You won't need to marry; you'll earn your own living." Aunt Amalia put a hand to my cheek. "There are very few women who can choose to marry or not as it pleases them. You're a fortunate girl indeed. Besides, you were born to be a physician. It was written in the stars."

Those words became my truth. I knew two things from that day forward: I would not marry, and I would be a physician.

As the night wears on, memories of Eneko and our evenings of passion surge into my mind like crashing waves. I can still feel the warmth of his mouth on mine, see the gleam of delight in his eyes when I moan in pleasure under his touch. Now I feel caged in our rented lodgings, my desire for him like a throbbing wound.

The next morning, I rise as soon as dawn breaks. I've

barely slept. Rosetta lies unmoving on her side of the bed, so deeply asleep that I have to shake her awake.

"My head aches," she mumbles, half opening her eyes. "If it's all the same to you, signorina, I'll stay abed."

I put a hand on Rosetta's forehead. It is warm, but not alarmingly so. I pull up her sleeve and reassure myself that the scar on her arm is healing well, thanks to my nettle remedy in Mdina.

"I'm going to Aunt Amalia's home again," I tell her. "I won't let that servant turn me away today."

"But you should wait for Beñat," Rosetta protests.

"I know where I'm going, and this is a respectable neighborhood. There are almonds in here." I place a small leather pouch next to Rosetta's head. "And there's watered wine in the pitcher on the table. Do you want some now?"

Rosetta makes a face. "No. I want to sleep."

"As you wish. But you must latch the door behind me."

She rolls out of bed with a groan and follows me to the door. "May the saints watch over you, signorina. I'll say a prayer for your safe return."

Slipping through the doorway, I wait to hear her slide the latch into place. Rosetta's muttered prayer seeps under the door into the corridor, following me to the staircase and down the steps.

I greet the landlady and set off into the chilly morning air, bolstered by a mixture of determination and nervous anticipation. Imagining the warmth of Aunt Amalia's embrace, I stride ever faster up the hill toward her house, a smile tugging at my lips.

CHAPTER 22

I ENTER the square where Aunt Amalia's home stands, swathed in its black bands of mourning cloth. Near the entrance to the palazzo-turned-bank opposite the house, a group of well-dressed men is gathered in a knot. Another pair of men wearing short black capes and matching caps approaches the group from across the square. An uneasy feeling takes hold of me. Something about one of the two men strikes me as familiar. I observe his stolid, measured gait, the tilt of his head, the width of his shoulders. Eneko's words come back to me in a rush:

There will be Florentine merchants in the city for the wool market.

What if Signor Lucchesi is here?

I force myself to keep walking at the same pace and melt into a nearby lane. Slipping into the shadows, I pull my cloak tight and tug the hood low over my brow, keeping my gaze fixed on the pair of men.

Surely, Signor Lucchesi wouldn't have pursued me to Genoa. After all, what use would it be for a man of his wealth to bother with a woman of no means? He took my inheritance, my home, my possessions. He could have no use for me now. No, if he is in Genoa, he must be here for the wool market, like so many other merchants whose ships are anchored in the harbor.

Unless he is a vindictive man who will stop at nothing to prosecute a broken contract.

I remember the cold gleam in his eyes, the threatening words he uttered in the lawyer's office. His anger in Salerno's harbor when I defied his order to return to shore.

Yes, I realize. Signor Lucchesi is *exactly* that kind of man.

The group of men outside the bank rebuffs the overtures of the newcomers. They don't seem to be acquainted, after all.

Is one of them Signor Lucchesi or not? They're too far off. I can't be certain.

The two black-caped fellows walk away, their retreating backs diminishing step by step, and then vanish into a busy lane.

On wobbly knees, I hurry to the church by the square. The stale air inside the church smells of incense. Several women kneel before the altar, the gentle clack of their rosary beads audible.

I approach the altar, genuflect, and say a silent prayer for the salvation of Uncle Dante's soul. My stomach growls. The church bells mark the hour with hollow, solemn clangs.

Walking back along the nave, I glance at the women perched on benches in the flickering candlelight. None of them return my gaze . . . until the last one. She pushes aside her mourning veil and regards me with slate-blue eyes. My heart lurches with hope.

"Aunt Amalia?" I ask, my voice as high and thin as a girl's.

She is stouter, and her face has more lines than a decade ago. But her eyes are unchanged, and the kindness I see there makes me burst into tears.

As I struggle to contain my sobs, Aunt Amalia stands and throws her arms around me.

"Come, *cara* Giuliana," she whispers in my ear. "Let us return to my home."

When we enter her house, the manservant who refused to admit us yesterday surveys me with a disapproving stare.

"Is this truly your niece, signora?" he asks my aunt.

She gives him a sharp look. "Of course she is. Have refreshment sent to my parlor at once. Wine, almond cakes, sheep's cheese, and fruit."

He stalks away, scowling.

"The steward thinks of himself as the man of the house now," Aunt Amalia says. "My husband told him to protect me, and he takes his instructions a bit too seriously."

"I see."

Though I understand his impolite behavior a little better now, I still find the man mean-spirited.

In her parlor, a maid takes my cloak and offers me a bowl of rose water to wash my hands in, along with a rose-scented linen towel. After we've both washed our hands, Aunt Amalia embraces me again, teary-eyed. She leads me to a cushion-topped stool near a window and tosses another cushion on the oak chair next to it, then sinks down with a sigh.

I take both her hands in mine. "I'm sorry your husband has died and made you a widow again."

"He was a good man," she says wistfully. "He never struck me or spoke to me unkindly. He taught me much about the business of buying and selling wool, and his reserves of patience were boundless. But I did not realize how generous a heart he had until he died." She trails off, her eyes glittering with tears, and puts a hand to my cheek. "This is a welcome surprise indeed. What a gift to see you, my precious niece. But why did you not write and tell me of your visit? And why hasn't my brother accompanied you?"

I take in a deep breath. "I regret to tell you of another great loss, but I can't wait any longer." I withdraw the leather cord and remove the ring. "Uncle Dante gave this to me the day he died. He said I must deliver it to you, and I've longed for this moment ever since."

Aunt Amalia slips the ring on, raises it to her lips, and kisses it. Her breath is shaky, and for a time she says nothing.

Another servant enters with our wine and food, and we sit in silence as he serves us. When he closes the door upon leaving the parlor, Aunt Amalia returns her gaze to the ring.

"This belonged to our father and his father before him," she says. "I will treasure it. There is no one to carry on the line, not anymore."

"I suppose I might have a son one day, though I doubt it very much." I think of Eneko when I say that.

Aunt Amalia looks at me. "Even if you did have a son, the line would still be dead."

"Why?"

Her face twists in an odd, conflicted expression, then smooths again. "Because you're not a Rinaldi, *cara* Giuliana. Dante never wanted to tell you the truth of your origins, but you deserve to know. He created the story that you are the child of our other sister. We had no other sister."

"Who is my mother, then?" I manage to ask. "And my father?"

"The great Trotula de Ruggiero was your ancestress. That is all I know. My brother said raising you was an honor he took on willingly and with utmost devotion. He was determined to help you follow in her footsteps, even though it is much more difficult today for women to do so."

My heart must be beating; my lungs must be drawing in

air. Yet as I absorb Aunt Amalia's words, I feel completely detached from my body. They *had* been words, hadn't they? Not cannons exploding the earth under my feet, not flames consuming the timbers in this home. Yet their impact is so colossal the words might as well be giants stomping down Genoa's cobbled streets, splintering homes and crushing church spires.

"Perhaps I was abandoned," I say slowly. "Perhaps my parents didn't want me."

"If they'd wanted to abandon you, they wouldn't have gone to the trouble of placing you with Salerno's most skilled and respected physician. That was an act of love. And now you're a physician yourself. There is no greater tribute to your ancestors than that."

I almost correct her, then silence myself, recalling Eneko's faith in my abilities as a medical practitioner. I remember Signora Tarrag's insistence that if she told the world I was a physician, it would be so. My aunt looks at me and sees a physician, not a failed medical student. Why can't I, once and for all, do the same?

My mind reels as I try to conjure up my earliest recollections, searching for a trace of my parents in the distant past. Every time I catch hold of a memory, though, I find myself back in the kitchen with Rosetta, playing with rolled-up balls of dough by the hearth.

She must know something of this. Why did she never speak of it? To her, secrets are for sharing.

I chew my lip, mulling over my realization. Could it be that Rosetta is capable of more discretion than I'd ever imagined? I think of all the times I've felt impatient, even angry with Rosetta's wagging tongue. Shame creeps over my skin, igniting a flush in my cheeks. Rosetta has always loved me and looked after me. The truth is I've never expressed gratitude to her for all she's done to keep me safe and happy.

Aunt Amalia slides an arm around my shoulders and gently begins to question me about the events that have unfolded since Uncle Dante's death. After I explain the past few months of my tumultuous life—without elaborating on Malta, an experience I would rather forget—I confide my fear that Signor Lucchesi will track me down in Genoa.

"I thought I saw him outside the bank near your house," I admit.

"Many of the merchants in the Genoese wool guild use that bank. Sometimes foreign merchants bank there, too, but only at the invitation of a Genoese guild member. I can guess why he offered to bring you to Genoa each year. He wanted to insinuate himself into the wool guild here. Foreign merchants must lodge together and are only allowed into the city for short periods. But family connections grease the wheels of commerce and loosen the rules. He had his eye on reduced tariffs, better terms for wool trading, a well-situated stall at the wool merchant's market, and the like."

"How do you know all of this?" I ask, impressed with her knowledge.

"I often attended the guild meetings with my husband, for he wanted me to understand the business so I might be prepared in the event of his death. I kept the accounts for him, and he wanted me to continue doing so whenever my stepsons are away from Genoa. It's written in his will."

"Truly?"

"Truly. His will held other surprises, too. The pilgrimage to Jerusalem he was meant to take has been paid for. There's a fine cabin in a merchant vessel reserved. The fleet of ships will stop in Rhodes, Cyprus, Alexandria . . ."

"But he won't be able to take the journey. Can you get the money back?"

Aunt Amalia chuckles. "Of course not. The will stipulated that I should make the journey on his behalf should he die in advance of the pilgrimage. That way, I can pray for his soul's salvation at every stop along the journey. It's the only way to assure his passage into heaven."

"Do you wish to make this voyage?" I ask, surprised. "It will be long and dangerous."

"I've never wished more for anything, Giuliana. It will be the crowning glory of my life, this pilgrimage. A magnificent adventure."

An image of Eneko on the deck of his ship strikes me, his golden-brown eyes laughing, the sun lighting him from behind. He spoke of stopping in Rhodes, too, on his journey through the Eastern seas. A thrill of hope ripples through me as I entertain an audacious idea.

"There's only one thing missing from your plan, Auntie. A companion who will also serve as your personal physician in case of sickness or injury. To keep you comfortable and safe along the way."

She looks at me, uncomprehending for a moment, then a smile blooms on her face and she takes my hands in hers. "I'd consider it an honor to have you by my side."

CHAPTER 23

Aunt Amalia sends two young manservants with me to collect Rosetta and our belongings. I'm careful to keep my hood on in case Signor Lucchesi is indeed in these streets, but I'm bursting with excitement about the journey ahead and eager to question Rosetta about my parents.

Inside the lodging house, the landlady stops me at the entrance.

"Your servant had a visitor. That Basque fellow. And when she left with him, she was weeping."

The woman's voice has a hard edge to it, and whatever warmth had been in her eyes during our previous encounters has vanished.

"Rosetta left?" I ask in disbelief. "Was she hurt?"

"She walked on her own two feet, that's all I can tell you. Carrying a load of belongings. We can't have trouble here, signorina. This is a respectable house."

"Forgive me for any disturbance, signora. It will not happen again."

The woman's tight expression does not ease as I climb the stairs.

In our chamber, I search in vain for my possessions. I separated my money before leaving Eneko's galley and placed half in the satchel. But the satchel is nowhere to be found. Now half my money and all of my things have disappeared with Rosetta.

My mind catches on an image of Trotula's book, its water-stained pages, the indecipherable mess of its smeared words.

The loss of my ruined book hurts the most.

I sink down on the bed, stunned.

Rosetta would not steal from me. I am certain of it. She took my things to keep them safe because she was frightened or threatened. Surely, not by Beñat. He seems love-addled in her company, always trying to please her. And besides, Eneko trusts Beñat more than any other man in his crew. There must be some good reason for Rosetta to have left with him.

Downstairs, I ask the landlady to send Rosetta to Aunt Amalia's house in the event of her return.

Back at my aunt's home, I castigate myself for not learning the location of Beñat's lodging. I have no idea where he and his men are staying and no way of communicating with them. I pray he is as good a man as he seems, and I beg the saints to bring Rosetta back to me.

That night, I sleep poorly in a small but elegantly appointed bedchamber in my aunt's spacious home, tormented by worries about Rosetta.

The next morning, I send two servants out early to inquire at the lodging house about Rosetta, and they return with no news. As Aunt Amalia prepares to go out for meetings with her notary and lawyer, I try to convince her to let me come along.

"Please, Giuliana," she says, "Stay here and keep safe. That

Florentine and his men could be anywhere. If he accosts you in the streets, I may not be able to prevent him from taking you into his custody."

"But Rosetta needs me," I argue. "She's not feeling well, she's—"

The steward approaches from behind us, his footfalls nearly silent on the polished stone floor.

"Signora, when I went to the harbor this morning to purchase salted cod for your journey, I saw the signorina's servant and her Basque companion talking to a ship captain. They'll be off to Basqueland soon, no doubt. Back where they belong." His lip curls when he says that.

"What?" I burst out. "We need to find out where they're staying. Rosetta would never leave Genoa without me."

He is unmoved by my words. His dark eyes are like rain-slicked pebbles in his expressionless face.

I appeal to my aunt. "Can you please send him to the harbor again to search for their lodgings?"

"My steward must remain here while I'm out." She appraises him with a long look. "If a Florentine by the name of Lucchesi calls here, do not admit him. He's not to step foot in my home, is that understood?"

The steward nods stiffly. "As you wish, signora."

"And if my servant, Rosetta, calls, admit her at once," I admonish him, but he gives no indication that he's heard me.

When he walks away, Aunt Amalia says, "I'll send other servants to inquire at the waterfront about Rosetta and the Basques. We'll do our best to find them."

While she's gone, I give the parlor maid two silver coins and tell her there will be more if she alerts me every time a visitor raps on the front door. Then I busy myself in the parlor cutting and rolling lengths of linen for various uses during the journey. I secure a bundle with flax twine, then reach for more strips of cloth. Worries about Rosetta fill my mind.

I forced her to leave Salerno with me, assuaging her fears with lies about a safe future in Genoa. She has endured countless dangers since then—all because I was too proud to marry a wealthy merchant, too blinded by my dream of becoming a physician.

I drop the linen and cover my face with my hands, burning with shame. Part of me wants to rush outside and search the streets for Rosetta. But I don't know this city. I would be a fool to wander on my own.

I pray for her safety, then my mind strays to Eneko. Where is he now? The Greek island of Rhodes? The Kingdom of Cyprus? How long does it take to sail to those places?

My thoughts are interrupted by the soft voice of the parlor maid.

"Callers asking the steward for you, signorina."

I stop breathing for a moment, instantly on guard.

Please, God, let it not be Signor Lucchesi.

"Who is it?" Slowly, I rise, trying to keep my voice steady.

"A woman and a man. Humbly dressed. She says she works for you."

Rosetta!

I fly into the entry hall just as the door thumps shut. The steward and I lock eyes, and the triumphant look on his face makes me want to slap him. How dare he turn Rosetta away once again?

"Those callers aren't fit to enter this home," he says, putting up a hand as if that alone could keep me from my Rosetta.

"Move aside," I order him.

He stays where he is. I bat away his outstretched hand, and he moves to block me. I reach for my dagger, but of course it's not hanging from my belt. I'd removed it last night, assuming I would not need it in Aunt Amalia's home. How foolish of me.

I let my shoulders sag and bow my head, feigning sobs. From under my lashes, I see his stance loosen, his vigilance relax. He begins to turn away. I spring forward, push past him, and unlatch the door.

Rosetta and Beñat stand before me, gilded by the morning sun. The satchel is strung over Rosetta's shoulder, intact.

I sweep Rosetta across the threshold and embrace her fiercely.

The steward sidles between me and the door, fuming, and I gesture to Beñat to enter before he slams it shut again.

"What happened to you?" I ask finally, holding Rosetta at arm's length. "Why did you disappear? I've done nothing but worry!" Without waiting for a reply, I turn to Beñat. "Why did you take her away?"

"It was as you feared," he says soberly. "The Florentine wool merchant and his men were visiting lodging houses, offering money to anyone who would deliver you to him."

"So you took Rosetta under your wing but left me to fend for myself?" I can't help feeling indignant.

Rosetta takes my hand. "When you went to find your aunt yesterday morning, Beñat came to the lodging house. He told me to come and be quick about it, for the men were on our trail. I was so frightened! I gathered our things, and we hurried here to get you, only this man refused to let us in." She glares at the steward, whose disapproving expression darkens further.

"I was in the parlor with Aunt Amalia when they came here," I say to the steward, fuming. "And you said nothing of their visit!"

He pretends not to hear. Protectiveness is one thing, but this man seems to think he runs the house.

"Come into the parlor," I tell Rosetta and Beñat. "This man has a door to guard."

The steward gives me a sour look as we walk away.

Inside the parlor, Beñat pats Rosetta's arm in a gesture of unconscious tenderness. "She wasn't feeling well yesterday as it was, so I took her back to my quarters. As soon as she awoke today, she wanted to return here and find you."

Rosetta thrusts out the satchel, and I assess the objects within. Everything is as I placed it. I rest my gaze on the ruined book, giving a silent prayer of thanks for its return.

"Did my uncle ever tell you anything about my mother and father?" I ask her.

She stills, a guarded look on her face. "He said never to speak of it."

"I know the truth now," I say. "There's no need to be secretive any longer."

"Then you finally see why you were meant to be a physician, signorina!" She smiles. "It's in your blood!"

"How did you keep that to yourself all these years?" I ask her. "Gossiping is your favorite pastime, after all."

"Is that a warning to me?" Beñat asks, raising an eyebrow.

Rosetta lightly slaps his arm. "I *can* keep a secret if it's important enough."

"It's true." I look at her with new respect. "You've kept your vow to Uncle Dante. But I still don't understand why it was so important to him that the world believed I was a Rinaldi, too."

"I do." Rosetta continues in a hushed, sober tone. "Your mother was newly widowed when you were a babe. She worked as a physician day and night to support her household. One day, she was accused of witchcraft by the husband of a woman who had died in childbirth under your mother's watch. A priest spread the story around the city, and soon other families came forward blaming her for their own troubles. All lies, of course."

"Was she burned at the stake?" I can barely breathe. "Killed by a mob?"

Rosetta shakes her head. "She got terribly ill in the midst of all this, and your uncle cared for her. Before she died, she asked him to raise you as his own niece and take his name so you wouldn't be a target of cruelty from those who hated her. Everything Signor Dante did from that day forward was for your protection."

I cannot speak. My entire being seems distilled down to my aching heart.

"What's wrong?" Rosetta asks in alarm. "Are you in pain, signorina?"

"Not at all," I assure her once I can speak again. "In fact, I wish to invite you on a journey. My aunt will make a pilgrimage to the Holy Land, with me as companion. Will you accompany us?"

Rosetta's smile fades. "Heavens, no. I can't stomach another sea voyage. I want to keep my feet planted on the ground."

"In Genoa? You know nobody here. Where will you find work?"

Beñat clears his voice. "She'll lodge with me. I have plenty of coin, and when Captain Eneko returns, I'll have more."

I give him a skeptical look. "Truly?"

He nods. "He's generous with his best men, and I'm not too humble to say I'm one of them. I carry out his business for him when he's at sea, and I haven't disappointed him yet."

Rosetta's eyes are on Beñat, and the adoration I see in them warms my spirit.

"We get along, that's all," she says. "We're a good fit."

Beñat chuckles. "In more ways than one." He busses her on the cheek, and she dissolves in giggles.

I regard the pair of them thoughtfully, trying to absorb the reality of my servant's new situation. Under Beñat's teasing gaze, Rosetta's eyes shine, and a rosy glow illuminates her cheeks. One thing is undeniable: she has never looked happier.

"What if Beñat sails back to Basqueland once Eneko returns to Genoa?"

Rosetta looks alarmed. "Would you, Beñat?"

"I might not have a choice, Rosie. Captain's orders can't be refused. But you'd be welcome among the Basques. A woman who can cook like you is held in high regard."

She chews her lip, brow furrowed. "It would mean a sea voyage, though."

"You may not enjoy it, but you do well on the seas," I remind her. "Better than most folk."

Rosetta lets out an agonized sigh, then throws up her hands. "I'll go, as long as I can be with Beñat."

He draws her into his embrace. "Wherever you go, I'm at home, Rosie."

CHAPTER 24

WHEN WE ARRIVE at the harbor on the day of our departure, a strong wind is gusting—just as it had the day Uncle Dante died. I pull my hood low and keep a firm grip on my satchel, unsettled despite the comforting presence of Aunt Amalia and her servants. Along with several other ships destined for the East, the Genoese galley we'll board for the journey is anchored close to the docks. Already, passengers and their luggage are being transported from the shore to the ship in grippos that move briskly through the choppy waters.

The captain himself greets passengers and examines their possessions with a practiced eye. Most of the travelers have brought extra food and drink, as we have. Many also carry pillows, featherbeds, and rugs to make their spartan quarters more inviting.

Aunt Amalia exchanges pleasantries with the captain while the servants unload our traveling cases and other items from the donkey cart.

I take in the activity around me, fascinated by the objects on display. A man has brought a rectangular writing desk with cleverly constructed legs folded up underneath it. A few people carry pets in cages, including ferrets and cats. One woman has a wooden cabinet filled with precious leather-bound books, three wool fleeces tied with twine, an entire set of armor, and six casks of wine. When I admire the armor, she explains that her son is a knight of the Order of St. John on Rhodes, and she is determined to ensure he survives the experience.

The captain's assistant notes each item on a sheet of parchment attached to a thin board. Another man holds the inkwell for him as he dips the nib and scratches out the words. Occasionally the captain demands extra payment for particularly heavy or bulky items.

As Aunt Amalia supervises the loading of our luggage into a grippo, someone tugs at my sleeve. I turn, startled, to see the beaming faces of Beñat and Rosetta. Beñat has a package wrapped in canvas under his arm.

"We came to see you off," Rosetta cries. "Hurry, now, Beñat. Give it to her!"

He gives her an indulgent smile and hands the package to me.

I weigh the hard, rectangular object in my hands, mystified. "You got me a book, Beñat?"

"Not just any book," Rosetta says. "Your favorite book."

The noise and activity of the busy port falls away as I carefully unwrap the canvas. The leather cover is embossed with faded gilt tracery. I lift it with care and study the words on the title page, my pulse quickening.

"Trotula's book on the ailments of women," I say in wonder, raising my gaze to Beñat. "You found another copy?"

"There are more than you'd think, for Trotula's fame spread widely during her life and beyond," my aunt says, looking over my shoulder. "I tried to find you a copy, too. The one I had my eye on was sold out from under me, though. The buyer was a foreigner."

She gives Beñat a pointed stare.

He shrugs, spreading his hands wide in a gesture of innocence. "I was only doing my captain's bidding."

I turn to Beñat. "Eneko told you to buy me this?"

"'Watch over her and find her another copy of that blasted book,' he said before sailing away."

Rosetta harrumphs. "He likely said 'blessed book,' *caro* Beñattino."

Beñat grins at the reprimand or perhaps at the term of endearment. "Aye, you're right, Rosie."

At that moment, two men rush to Beñat's side, speaking in rapid Basque. His expression tightens.

"That wool merchant," he says to me. "He's on the docks searching for you, thanks to his informant."

"Who is his informant?" I ask, my mouth going dry.

"Your aunt's steward. I've had my men follow him the past several days. This morning, he went straight to the Florentine's lodging house as soon as you and your aunt left for the harbor. That wool merchant is lining his purse with gold."

Shaken, I envelop Rosetta in an embrace. "Thank you," I whisper in her ear. "I'll always carry you in my heart." Turning to Beñat, I implore, "Take good care of her."

He nods. "I plan to, signorina."

"In we go." I steer Aunt Amalia to the grippo.

A gull screams overhead. Behind us, a man's voice rings out, heralding the captain.

"I am Antonio Lucchesi, merchant of Florence. I'm certain that my betrothed is among your passengers," he booms. "She must be returned to my care at once."

My knees nearly gave way. With the aid of a crewman, I step aboard, then extend a hand to Aunt Amalia. We both sink down on a bench on the far side of the boat.

"What's the lady's name, then?" the captain demands.

"Giuliana Rinaldi." Signor Lucchesi enunciates my name with slow precision.

Our two servants, a young woman and her brother, board the grippo. Aunt Amalia directs them to sit between me and the docks, creating a human shield.

I strain to hear the captain's response. The boat teeters from side to side, unstable in the shifting waters. Finally, the captain's voice rises up.

"Nobody by that name on this galley," he announces.

"Show me your roster, Captain!" Signor Lucchesi insists.

I tap on a crewman's shoulder, gesturing at the oars. "Row!" I plead.

But he stays motionless, enthralled by the drama unfolding on the dock.

"See for yourself," the captain retorts. "There is a female passenger named Giuliana on this roster, but her surname is not Rinaldi. It's de Ruggiero."

Aunt Amalia squeezes my hand.

"Where is this woman called Giuliana?" the wool merchant cries.

"Enough, signor," the captain says in annoyance. "Giuliana is a common name. You're not a citizen of Genoa, I've never met you before, and you have no standing to take a passenger off my ship."

A buzz of excitement ripples through the crowd.

One of the crewmen on the grippo shades his eyes. "The Florentine just tossed the captain a purse. A fat one, too."

Only the warm pressure of Aunt Amalia's hand keeps me breathing.

"I showed you the courtesy of sharing my roster with you, signor," the captain says. "And now you resort to a bribe? Perhaps Florentines buy men's loyalty this way, but we do things differently in Genoa. Does my crew have to escort you off the docks, or will you leave peacefully?"

Signor Lucchesi's response is inaudible in the rising commotion of passengers and crew readying to board the fleet of vessels.

"Nothing more to see," the crewman reports, taking his seat by the oarlock and slipping his oar into place.

As we glide toward the galley, I squeeze Aunt Amalia's hand in relief.

"That was your doing," I say.

My aunt leans close.

"The name on the roster was, but the captain's protection was not. When I brought my notary to his office to finalize the details for our voyage, the captain gave me a document showing proof of insurance for the journey. He said our passage to the Holy Land had already been generously insured."

"But who could have done that?" I'm baffled.

"A Basqueman went to the captain and insured our passage with gold. Said he was doing his master's bidding—he claimed he was under orders to protect you. His master's name started with an *E*."

"Eneko?" I offer slowly, shaking my head in disbelief.

"That's it. I'm assuming now the servant who conducted this business was Beñat. So you know this man, Eneko?"

I nod, dazed.

"Our captain also told me the Basques are the finest sailors at sea—but many of them are pirates." Her expression turns skeptical. "I find it hard to believe a pirate would go to the trouble and expense of insuring our passage to the Holy Land."

I can't help but smile. The dread that nearly crushed me moments ago vanishes, replaced by a growing sense of anticipation about the journey ahead.

"Even pirates can have generous spirits," I say softly. "Especially that one."

CHAPTER 25

A MONTH LATER

I LEAN out over the water, drumming impatient fingers on the galley's wooden railing. I'm near the navigator and the captain, and I catch snippets of their conversation as I study the foam-capped waves. The other ships in our fleet are so far away I can't see their banners. I count the vessels under my breath. One, two, three. Where's the fourth? The sun is low in the western sky, throwing light over the Mediterranean Sea's sapphire waves, and my eyes ache from searching.

After the storm we just endured, it's no surprise that our fleet has scattered in all directions.

Eneko once told me that in times of great duress, he prays to Mari, storm goddess of the Basques. The seafarers of Salerno pray to Santa Maria, but Eneko believes there is no force more powerful than Mari.

I trust his faith in the Basque goddess, but I also trust Santa Maria's power to protect those at sea. So I turn my face to the sky and say, "Santa Maria, Mari, I beg both of you, let the fleet close ranks again, and keep us safe until we arrive in Rhodes."

The gales of recent days have a bit of fight in them still, and the wind is pushing us east at a brisk pace. I watch, mesmerized, as the rest of the fleet approaches. The ships' red-and-white banners are visible now, rippling in the wind.

I only wish Aunt Amalia could be up here breathing the fresh air with me. But she's been struck down by seasickness more often than not on this journey. She endures it with stoic acceptance. I've done what I can for her with possets containing ginger root and my limited supply of herbs, knowing the only cure for her will be to stand on solid ground.

A crewman who scrambled up the mast earlier calls out, "Four vessels sighted, Captain!"

I smile with relief. All accounted for.

Thank you, Mari. Thank you, Santa Maria.

Three dolphins surface off the bow, their sleek bodies glistening under the bright sunlight. I cry out in delight at the sign of good fortune. My shout mingles with whoops of excitement from others on deck, and we cheer as the creatures burst from the waves again.

After a time, the man at the top of the mast bellows, "I see Rhodes, Captain!"

More cheers reverberate through the air, followed by a vigorous trumpet serenade and a round of enthusiastic piping from the stern.

"Did *everyone* aboard bring a pipe on this voyage?" the navigator grumbles. "They're loud enough to wake the dead."

I chuckle, grateful to have something to laugh about. The other ships in our fleet are so close now I can make out individual figures on board. A return barrage of trumpeting and wild piping breaks out on their decks, echoing thinly across the swells.

Soon Rhodes looms before us like a gold-green mountain pushing up from the waves, reaching for the sky. Most of the islands we've passed in recent days are much smaller, with settlements of white-washed homes and domed churches perched on craggy cliffs. As we approach the harbor, I see windmills along an enormous seawall, their blades slowly turning in the breeze. Massive stone walls encircle the hillside port city of Rhodes Town. A palace sits at the crest of the hill, overlooking the busy port below.

We enter the harbor, and the crew drops anchor while the trumpeters herald our arrival. There's a separate harbor nearby full of warships whose banners bear the mark of the Knights Hospitaller of the Order of St. John—a white eight-pointed cross on a black background. Small craft navigate around our galley, returning from the sea loaded with fish and squid. Gulls screech and circle overhead.

I descend below decks to help Aunt Amalia disembark. The captain has assured us he will stay in Rhodes Town for several days to make necessary repairs to the boat and gather all the supplies for the next leg of the journey. We'll lodge at a Genoese inn with other passengers on pilgrimage, in a respectable quarter of the city.

When I burst into our cabin, spilling details about all I've seen, I'm encouraged to see Aunt Amalia dressed and ready to leave, with our servants packing all her belongings into storage trunks.

Her face is thinner than it was before we left on this journey, for it's been a struggle to keep food in her belly. And her skin is pale after all these weeks hidden from the sun.

I take her hands in mine. "Once you're on firm ground with sunshine on your face, you'll feel much better."

"There's nothing I want more." She smiles wanly. "I don't care for feeling ill, but I'm glad to be on this pilgrimage, even more glad I'm with you."

The servants carry the luggage above decks and we follow. When we're finally settled in a grippo and rowing toward the docks, my gaze is caught again by the waving black-and-white banners of the warships in the knights' harbor. The movement of black and white together reminds me of Eneko's banners, with their black interlocking patterns on white backgrounds.

And then, my heart surging with excitement, I realize this is no trick of the wind. I tap on a crewman's shoulder, hope rising in my chest. "Signor, is that a Basque ship anchored in the knights' harbor?"

He peers where I'm pointing and nods. "Must be a privateer working for the knights. They sometimes anchor there."

A thrill runs through my body, a tingling rush of amazement and delight. It could be a different Basque ship, I remind myself. Perhaps they all have the same pattern on their banners. I bounce on my toes impatiently as the crewmen tie up the boat to the docks.

Aunt Amalia looks at me sideways. "Is something wrong, Giuliana?"

I swallow, try to contain myself. Before I can come up with an answer, we're helped off the boat by two Genoese crewmen. I support Aunt Amalia with an arm around her waist as she sways a little, adjusting to the earth beneath her feet.

Two young boys carrying a basket of squid approach and, in Greek-accented Genoese, offer to sell us the contents for a florin. The crewmen shoo them away, warning us that Rhodes Town is full of vendors intent on selling their wares to pilgrims at inflated prices.

"My appetite is returning," Aunt Amalia says. "If those boys had oranges in their basket instead of squid, I'd have been tempted."

Already, her color is normal again, and there's a glint of

humor in her eye that reassures me she is regaining her health with every passing moment. The servants bring our belongings up from another grippo, and two crewmen lead us to a donkey cart ready to take us to our lodging.

A wild urge grows in me to dash away and investigate the Basque ship. My heart is thumping hard against my ribs, and my breath comes in quick, short gasps, as if I've just climbed a steep hill.

I clamber into the donkey cart and settle on the bench next to Aunt Amalia, and as we roll through the massive sea gates leading into the city, I force myself to focus on this moment rather than be consumed by hope and imagination.

Now, I remind myself. What matters is *now*.

The cobbled streets of Rhodes Town throng with citizens in flowing silk and cotton clothing, the women's hair obscured with elegantly draped head wraps and some of the men wearing turbans. Many of the homes we pass are whitewashed with lime; others are made of fine stone with broad carved doors that conceal hidden courtyards within. We pass a gated garden bursting with lush plants, and I luxuriate in the wafting scent of jasmine.

When we arrive at the Genoese inn, I ask the innkeeper if Basques ever lodge here. He nods, nonplussed.

"We had a Basque sea captain here a fortnight ago, but he rented chambers nearby after a few days, said he wanted a quieter place to lodge."

"Do you recall his name?" I keep my voice low, but Aunt Amalia is busy with the servants and luggage and is out of earshot anyway.

"I called him 'Captain,' as befits his rank. Never learned his name."

After settling into our chambers, Aunt Amalia and I visit the nearby women's bathhouse and change into clean clothing. We dine in the lodging house's courtyard under an olive wood trellis covered with twining grapevines. We eat brazier-grilled fish and squid and saffron-scented rice studded with wild onions. Pistachios, almonds, oranges, and grapes round out the meal, and we're served honey-sweetened white wine that glides down my throat all too easily.

It's high summer and the sky is still bright, though the many churches in Rhodes Town have just struck nine bells. A trio of Greek musicians play and sing for us. I should be lulled into contented satiety like all the other pilgrims, but instead my body pulses with barely contained energy. I close my eyes and see that Basque ship in the harbor, banners fluttering in the wind.

Our Genoese ship captain joins us for a cup of wine. He says he's already eaten at a tavern around the corner from our inn, a well-kept establishment owned by Greeks.

"The Georgillas tavern attracts ship captains from all over the world," he tells us. "Tonight, I heard at least ten languages, including German, Arabic, and Basque."

I put down my cup with a thump. "Basque?"

He nods. "Yes, a Basque sea captain. He works for the knights as a privateer, I heard."

Another pilgrim cuts in, "Did you hear any Russian in the tavern, Captain? I'm told merchants come down from the Black Sea bearing fur and timber from Siberia . . ."

I stare at the captain as he answers, watching his lips move but aware only of my mounting excitement.

Then I turn to Aunt Amalia. "Will you excuse me, Auntie? There's something I must attend to."

She waits a moment before answering, searching my eyes with a thoughtful expression. "Only if you take my manservant along with you. I won't have you wandering these streets alone."

I agree and kiss her cheek. "I'll be back before dark."

She casts a wry glance at the sky. "You'd best hurry, then."

And I do. After slipping the manservant a silver coin, I'm hastening through the twilight to the Georgillas tavern, where music spills out into the warm evening air from behind the closed door.

I push it open, the young man at my heels, and take in the busy atmosphere with a hopeful gaze. The crowd is an interesting mixture of heavily bearded Greeks in flowing cotton tunics alongside merchants in doublets and hose, some of them accompanied by their wives, and an assortment of sea captains with sun-weathered faces.

"Can I tempt you with a cup of honey-sweetened wine?" a woman with arresting dark eyes asks me in Greek-accented Genoese. I nod gratefully, and when she fetches it for me she tells me this is her family's tavern. I ask if a Basque captain was here tonight, and she smiles.

"He's still here." She tilts her head toward the open courtyard, where a lush grapevine shelters several tables. A man sits with his back to us at one of the tables, and I think—I hope—I recognize the broad sweep of his shoulders. A flickering torch casts a pattern of shadow and light on his form, and my breath hitches in my throat.

Eneko.

I tell my companion to wait inside, and I slip into the courtyard in the gathering dusk.

"My love." I whisper the words, approach Eneko with tentative steps as if he's made of smoke, an apparition that might disappear in the next instant.

He turns his head at the sound of my voice, startled. Our eyes meet. His expression registers shocked surprise, and he passes a hand over his face as if to chase away a conjured image. But when he looks at me a second time, he seems to understand that I am truly standing before him in a tavern on the island of Rhodes, and a smile slowly emerges on his face. He stands, holds out his arms, and I hurtle into them.

I've dropped my cup, I'm weeping and laughing at the same time, and he's crushing me to his chest, nuzzling me until my hair comes loose, tumbling around my shoulders.

"I've dreamed of this moment every night since we parted," he murmurs. "Yet this feels like a dream, too. How can I be sure you're real?"

I kiss him instead of replying, offering the proof of my existence with warm, eager lips. He returns my kiss with a wild hunger that leaves me weak-kneed.

"I've come to Rhodes as a pilgrim's physician," I tell him when I've caught my breath. His eyes shine at me in the torchlight, and I drink in the sight of him, shivering with joy. "But I've given much thought to your offer, and I believe I've got the makings of a pirate's physician, after all. Once I've completed this pilgrimage, Captain Eneko, perhaps we can come to an arrangement."

His dazzling smile is all the answer I need.

And for the first time since Uncle Dante's death, I allow myself to think about tomorrow.

Ready for more? *You'll find excerpts of the novels in the Sea and Stone Chronicles on the next pages.*

ISLAND OF GOLD (PREVIEW)

PROLOGUE

Languedoc, France
1435

Cédric offered the falcon a strip of rabbit meat. Ignoring the tidbit, she retracted her neck low into her shoulders, plumped her feathers, and fixed him with a baleful glare.

"Still off your feed?" he asked softly. "What ails you, my girl?"

A low growl of thunder startled him. He glanced through the open door to the courtyard, where rain pummeled the cobblestones. The scent of rotting straw hung in the air. If only sunshine would break through the clouds and give the land a chance to dry out.

Then a familiar figure filled the doorway, jolting him out of his thoughts.

"Philippe," he said in surprise. "But you're early—"

"It's your father," his sword master replied, breathing hard. "He's wounded."

Cédric dropped the pouch of rabbit meat and pushed past Philippe. He broke into a run when he glimpsed a guard and a servant across the courtyard, carrying his father through the front doors of the main house.

Inside the great hall, he cleared the broad oak table near the hearth with one sweep of his arm. Pewter and crockery smashed against the tile floor. Quickly, the men settled Papa on the table and removed his leather cuirass and chain-mail shirt. A deep wound gaped at his lower abdomen, leaking blood. His moans reverberated to the rafters.

Cédric yanked an embroidered flax runner off a nearby chest. It was one of the few reminders of his mother left in the house since her death on his twelfth name-day, nearly four years ago. With trembling hands, he wrapped it around his father's waist. The mingled aromas of sweat and blood filled his nostrils.

"It was the *écorcheurs,*" said the guard, removing his helmet and running a hand through his matted hair. "They surprised us on the road back from the seminary."

"They took my purse, my boots, my belt," Papa managed to croak. "The ring off my finger. And ran me through with my own sword."

"Those devils. I'll kill them!" The words exploded from Cédric's lips without warning. Philippe pressed a restraining hand on his shoulder. His heart thrummed crazily against his ribs all the same.

A servant hurried in with a jug of wine.

"Where is Yves?" Cédric demanded, tying the ends of the cloth together to bind his father's wound. The faint outlines of pink silk roses embroidered by his mother vanished under a relentless tide of scarlet blood. His eyes burned with tears at the sight.

"Your brother went to check on the mill this morning,"

Philippe said, accepting a cup of wine from the servant. "I've sent someone to fetch him. And the priest."

Cédric propped up his father's head and held the cup to his lips. He spluttered and coughed, then swallowed a bit of wine. A gust of wind and rain swept through the open doorway, the flames in the hearth dancing in response.

"These cursed rains," Papa muttered. "There will be no harvest this year."

Cédric stared at the fire, refusing to watch death tighten its grip on his father.

"And bandits circling like wolves." Philippe's voice was steady, but it held a trace of anger.

Papa sucked in a ragged breath. "My boy, look at me."

Cédric dragged his gaze from the hearth with reluctance.

"Yves will take my place as viscount. Stéphane is safe at seminary, his path to priesthood is secure. But you—" His father struggled for air, grimacing. "God forgive me, I've not prepared you, Cédric. You care more for falcons than swordplay. You're not ready to enter service for a *seigneur* . . ."

Philippe leaned closer. "I swear to you as a servant of the Knights Hospitaller that your son has the makings of a strong fighter. I'll be sure his training is complete before he enters any lord's household, my friend."

Papa sought Cédric's eyes again. "You can change your fate, but not if you spend your life bowing to the whims of other men, understand? One day you must make your own fortune."

The worry and pain in his expression made Cédric's heart twist.

"Vow it to me, son."

"I vow it." Cédric tried to swallow, but his throat felt dry as dust.

Papa's face relaxed. His breath grew faint, his skin pale.

"You will make your own way in the world," he whispered. "But first you'll learn to live by your sword—and stay alive."

Chapter 1

Summer, 1439
Auvergne, France

The thudding of dozens of hooves sounded on the road. Cédric put a hand in the air, motioning for silence. The men all exchanged somber glances. One of them crossed himself, then whispered to his horse in low tones. Cédric held his horse's bridle with one hand and clenched the hilt of his sword with the other. He glanced at the mule cart sitting in the shade of a hawthorn tree. It slowed their progress immeasurably. But there was no other choice. His entire future was bound up in that cart's cargo.

The riders began to pass by, shouting amongst themselves. The creak of leather, the metallic clank of swords, the snorting of horses filled the air. Cédric tightened his grip on his sword. He thanked God the weather had been dry this past week. The road here was hard-packed and dusty. Their presence would not be easily read in muddy furrows and hoofprints.

The approaching horses slowed.

Had the bandits seen something? Heard something?

God save us.

Then he distinctly heard one of them shout, "To the ferry!"

The hoofbeats quickened, the group sweeping down the roadway to the north, toward the river. He had bribed the ferryman to stay quiet about their passage when they'd crossed that river at dawn, but could only hope the man would keep his promise.

"We're nearly to the commandery," he told the men after a few tense moments of silence, climbing into the saddle again. "We'll arrive tonight, God willing."

"If we aren't skinned alive first," one of his companions retorted, fear still plain on his face.

"We've made it this far," Cédric said. "All the way from Bruges. We'll get there with our skins attached, fear not. And then you'll get your portion."

"How do we know we'll be safe there?" the man challenged him. "That band of rogues may have laid siege to the place this morning."

Cédric shot him a hard look. "The knights will not be bested by a pack of bandits, of that you can be sure. No more talk. Let's move out!"

As they rode back into the sun and headed south toward the rolling hills of central Auvergne, he hoped his claim was true. The commandery, like all possessions of the Knights Hospitaller, was strongly fortified and protected by skilled soldiers. But the *écorcheurs* were trained fighters as well, many of them mercenaries who had worked for powerful lords in the past.

A crow's raucous call in the woods to his left startled him back to the journey at hand. The lump of dread in his gut hardened with each turn of the cart wheels. Neither he nor any of his companions could resist glancing over their shoulders constantly as the day progressed, and they spurred their tired mounts forward with muttered promises of grain and hay.

They arrived at the commandery before nightfall, just as he'd hoped. Their exhausted horses plodded through the great iron-studded doors into the courtyard, where torches burned at intervals along the walls. A cloaked figure approached across the cobblestones.

"Cédric?"

In the wavering light, Cédric made out the familiar face of his father's dearest friend.

"Philippe!" Somehow he found the energy to spring down from his mount and embrace the sword master.

Stablehands emerged from the shadows as the other men dismounted.

The doors clanged shut behind them. For the first time in many days, Cédric drew a deep breath.

"I can't tell you how relieved I am to be here," he said to Philippe.

"Your cargo is sound?" Philippe nodded at the cart.

The mules pulling it looked ready to collapse.

"Fortune was kind on our journey," Cédric allowed.

Philippe turned to the other men. "Go inside. There's hot stew awaiting you, and we'll have water heated for baths."

"First I must take the falcons to the mews," Cédric said, though a hot meal and a bath sounded immeasurably better. Still, what was the point of transporting the birds all that way only to lose sight of them at the last?

Philippe nodded. "I'll come with you."

The other men collected their panniers and followed a servant through the commandery's inner doors.

Slinging an arm over Philippe's shoulders, Cédric smiled a little. "Why we're not dead on the roadside is a mystery."

"A mystery?" Philippe pointed at the heavens as they walked toward the stables and mews, a stablehand leading the mule cart behind them. "God was watching over you."

Cédric cast a glance at his surroundings, taking in the stone chapel and the other buildings that faced the central courtyard. An atmosphere of hushed prosperity and organization emanated from the carefully tended property.

"The knights live well," he observed. "How do you like your lot here?"

"Square meals, hot baths, quiet evenings. It can get a bit dull, to be honest. Nothing like my years working for the knights in Rhodes. But that was a young man's game."

"Dull sounds appealing at the moment," Cédric confessed. "I've longed for a quiet night since we left Bruges."

In the mews, Cédric and Philippe unloaded the wooden traveling cages and settled them in a secure, dry corner.

"Are their eyes seeled?" Philippe asked as Cédric withdrew the canvas coverings from the cages.

Cédric nodded. The hooded gyrfalcons, secured to their perches with leather jesses, barely stirred. "It was done in Norway before we left for the open seas."

He'd helped the Norwegian do the job, carefully stitching the falcons' eyelids shut with needle and thread. The stitches wouldn't be removed until the birds reached their final destination.

"Is there an under-falconer on duty here tonight?" he asked.

Philippe nodded, pointing at the dim figure of a man at the far end of the mews, who raised his hand in greeting. "He's seasoned, knows how to tend to these creatures."

"Are my father's birds healthy?" It was far too dark in here to get a good look at them now, Cédric realized.

"Just as they should be," Philippe assured him.

"You saved us, you know. If you hadn't persuaded the Order to buy Papa's falcons—"

"I only did what an old friend does for those he loves," Philippe said gruffly.

Together they walked out of the mews.

The other men had already eaten their fill in the refectory and retreated to the bathhouse. Cédric and Philippe sat at the end of a long table illuminated by several candles and the flames of a small fire in the hearth.

Cédric guzzled his wine and fell upon his bowl of mutton-and-barley stew as if he'd not eaten in days. Philippe ate nothing, just sipped from his own cup. Finally, when Cédric put down his spoon, he felt Philippe's eyes on him and glanced up.

"You must have a hundred questions." He poured himself another cup of wine.

"Not quite that many." Philippe's grizzled face twisted in a smile. "But a few, yes. You were gone longer than I imagined. I feared the worst. It was reckless of you, making this journey." He leaned forward, his expression hardening. "An enormous gamble."

"I was ready for it. Thanks to you."

"I had nothing to do with your survival. As I already said, you have God to thank for that."

"Not true," Cédric protested. "I never would have found a place in a *seigneur*'s household after Papa died without the blade skills you taught me. Surely, you can admit that."

"Swordplay always came naturally to you, even as a boy. And you've got courage. A bit too much of it, if we're honest." Philippe chuckled.

"Courage, maybe. But not luck. I chose the wrong man to work for in the end."

Philippe shook his head. "The *seigneur* died because of his own pride. He should have stayed within the keep of his castle rather than ride out to meet the *écorcheurs*. It was a tactical mistake."

"They were burning and raiding the villages on his lands! Wouldn't you have done the same?"

The sword master regarded Cédric thoughtfully for a moment. "When you consider what you came home to, perhaps fortune wasn't so unkind after all. Your family needed you."

Cédric fell silent, reflecting on his friend's words. He had retreated to the family lands after his employer's death with only the clothes on his back, a horse, and a sword. He had discovered his brother in debt, the mill providing much of their income rendered useless because of too many years without decent harvests.

"Perhaps you're right," he admitted.

"Indeed. You got your father's falcons safely here and kept the debtors at bay." Philippe pinned him with a glare. "Why you had to go chasing dreams in the North Sea is beyond me. Though I knew you had more chance of surviving the journey than most. Your time with the *seigneur* was exactly what you needed. There's a difference between swordplay and fighting for your life."

"Let's not forget who came up with the idea of big rewards for fulfilling a rich man's wishes," Cédric pointed out. "No one forced you to tell me the Count of Chambonac desired gyrfalcons."

"Just because a nobleman says he wants rare birds doesn't mean you should travel all the way to Norway to get them," Philippe said drily.

"Fair enough." Cédric shifted his weight on the bench. "What news of the count, anyway?"

Philippe put down his cup. "He snaps up castles like a wolf seizes deer in its jaws. Another one fell to him in the spring. But he is more merciful than some noblemen. He allowed the lady of the castle to bury her husband instead of putting his head on a pike. His new residence was completed not long ago, and the gossips say it's built entirely of pink stone."

"Will he honor his bid to pay handsomely for these falcons, do you think?"

"Nobles are an unpredictable bunch," Philippe said, shrugging. "One thing is certain, though. They all covet the falcons of the north. When you call upon the Count of Chambonac, whatever the outcome, I shall be at your side."

"But you're needed here," Cédric objected. "Trust me, I've survived enough violence for several lifetimes in the past few years. No matter what I encounter on the roads of Auvergne, I can fend for myself."

Cédric studied his old sword master in the flickering candlelight. His weathered skin was scored with fine cracks and lines, but he was still a formidably strong man. And the stubborn set of his jaw was all too familiar.

"Agreed," Philippe said, meeting his gaze. "But until those gyrfalcons are handed off properly, you can count on my sword just the same."

SEA OF SHADOWS (PREVIEW)

Summer, 1459
Rhodes Town

Anica Foscolo hurried through a crowd gathering in the marketplace under the blazing sun, trailed by her slave, Maria. All around them, traders unloaded their goods from donkey carts. The sugar sellers up the hill had already attracted a swarm of customers.

"Let's stop at the sugar stalls on the way back," she told Maria over her shoulder. "I want to make a lemon tonic for Mamá."

Maria nodded, stone-faced. She had not wanted to come on this errand, and she was never one to put on a false smile.

Two spice merchants leading heavily-laden donkeys ambled into their path, sending whiffs of cinnamon, ginger, and cloves into the air. Slowing her pace, Anica caught sight of a ceramics trader setting out bowls on a nearby table.

"Good day," she greeted him, moving closer.

Placing a hand over his heart, the man smiled in recognition. "When will your family return to Archangelos, signorina? It's been too long."

"Perhaps this autumn we'll be back." Anica traced the outline of a dolphin on a bowl with her fingertip, unwilling to explain the reason for their absence. "You're using blue paint for your designs now, like the Italians?"

His smile fading, he bent to rummage in a pannier filled with crockery. "Latins don't care for the Greek style. They want what they can get in Genoa or Florence, and they pay well for it."

At the mention of Florence, she tightened her grip on the canvas-wrapped parcel tucked under one arm and turned away.

There was no avoiding the Kastellania, where onlookers congregated at the whipping post as two guards hauled a chained inmate from the building's interior. Anica swallowed hard and sped her step, the prisoner's cries echoing in her ears. For the first time all morning, Maria matched her pace. The girl had always been terrified by the sight of a public flogging.

When they reached the Florentine banker's home, Maria hung back again, scowling.

"A slave is safer in the streets than in that man's house," she said in a voice dripping with venom.

"He's not your master," Anica retorted. "Come inside with me. All will be well."

Maria shook her head and stood her ground, refusing to meet Anica's eyes.

"If you prefer to broil in the sun, so be it." Anica regarded the polished cypress wood doors, wishing for her father's comforting presence. Then she drew in a breath, steeled herself, and lifted the heavy iron door knocker.

Signor Salviati kept her waiting in the high-ceilinged parlor for what seemed like an hour before he emerged from an adjoining chamber.

He approached, his silk tunic rustling. "Signorina," he said in a clipped voice, his expression cool. "I am eager to see your father's work."

Anica unwrapped the painting and presented it to him. It was exactly what he had asked for: a portrait of the Madonna and her child. The Virgin's shimmering blue robe, made of lapis lazuli pigment, had cost a small fortune. The banker held the panel at arm's length, pursing his lips. A long moment of silence passed. Anica's left knee began to tremble.

Finally, he spoke. "Exquisite." When he smiled, his graying teeth showed evidence of too many years' enjoyment of red wine. "Signor Foscolo is indeed a talented man. He shows much discipline, working to this standard even while he mourns his son. Although it has been some time since your brother's death, I suppose—"

"Six months today," Anica said shortly.

Since Benedetto's death, Anica had fought back her own sorrow and finished her father's commissions one by one. She'd sourced the pigments, prepared the panels, and layered on the tempera paints herself. From the backgrounds to the most intricate details of a shining eye or a silken sleeve, she was responsible for it all. But Signor Salviati would never know that.

A young, clean-shaven man also clothed in silk entered the parlor and came to stand at Signor Salviati's side.

"Ah! Troilo, look at the painting." The banker tilted the panel in the newcomer's direction. "Lovely, isn't it?"

The young man gave the painting a cursory inspection. Then his deep-set brown eyes fixed on Anica. "Not as lovely as you, signorina."

Signor Salviati lifted an eyebrow, his smile deepening. "Do you remember Troilo, my eldest son, signorina?"

She eyed the young man, who was a stocky, fleshy-faced version of his father. The Salviati family attended Santa Maria, where she often worshipped with Papa. But if she'd ever interacted with Troilo as a child, she had no recollection of it. "Yes, of course I do," she lied smoothly.

"We've both grown up since I was last in Rhodes," Troilo said. "You speak Italian as beautifully as if you'd been born and raised in Venice instead of Rhodes Town."

"My father did not overlook my education," she replied.

"He's a true citizen of Venice, then?" The banker's son narrowed his eyes. "Or a white Venetian?"

Anica stood taller. "He comes by his citizenship naturally —he did not buy it, I assure you."

"You're fortunate to possess some Latin blood, signorina," he said with a thin smile. "Though some might mistake you for Greek." He flapped a dismissive hand at her long cotton headpiece.

She felt the sting of shame, followed by a wave of anger. With effort, she kept her face impassive.

"Her mother is a Georgillas," Signor Salviati put in. "One of the first families."

When the Knights Hospitaller took ownership of Rhodes generations ago, a handful of Greeks had forged lucrative alliances with them. Mamá's family was descended from one of those men.

"Indeed?" his son said in a slightly more respectful tone.

Anica repressed an impatient sigh, eager to receive her payment and flee. Her gaze fell to the coin purse on Signor Salviati's belt. "My father expects me back straightaway."

He gave a start, one hand going to his waist. "Oh, he did not tell you? We've made other arrangements for payment. I shall not be giving you any coin today."

Anica studied the Florentine's face with suspicion. Her father had said nothing of this, but in his current state Papa could not be counted on to communicate anything of importance. She thought of the ducats she'd spent on pigments and other supplies to create this painting, of the expenses her family had faced for Benedetto's funeral. Words of protest rose up in her throat, but she gritted her teeth and pushed them back down again.

Speak with Papa first, she counseled herself. Keep this encounter pleasant, for his sake.

So rather than protest, she gave a quick curtsy. "Thank you, signor."

The younger Salviati put up a hand. "Wait." He plucked the wooden panel from his father's grasp. "I've spent the last five years in Florence, signorina. I saw dozens of portraits hanging in the finest homes there. Portraits of the men who've made their fortunes in wool and wine, done in a new style, with paints of oil."

"Oil?" repeated Signor Salviati.

His son nodded. "It's a style that started in the north. Flanders, I believe." He stepped closer to Anica. "Surely, you've heard of this?"

Anica resisted the urge to edge away. There was a wide space between his two front teeth. His pink tongue protruded slightly through the gap, and his breath smelled of fish and garlic.

"No," she said. "Artists use egg to thin the pigments. That is how it's always been done."

He shook his head. There was a hint of triumph in his expression. "Things are changing," he told her. "Oils are the new fashion. Your father had better learn this new style, or he shall soon find himself out of work."

Signor Salviati turned a sour expression on the panel that he had complimented a few moments before.

"If that is the case, then we shall have portraits made in oil, too. One of me, one of you, and one of your mother." The two men exchanged a satisfied look. Then the banker turned back to Anica. "Tell your father of my wish, Signorina Foscolo. He'll welcome the commission, I have no doubt."

Something in his tone sent a stab of worry into Anica's chest. "I will tell him, signor."

When a manservant let her out the front doors, she found Maria standing still as a statue where she'd left her, face covered with a sheen of sweat.

They pressed against the wall as a donkey cart piled with fruit rolled by. Anica looked back at the banker's home, her eyes aching from the glare of the sun against the white marble façade.

She should have been glad for another commission from the man. But instead, she felt certain no good would come of it.

THE QUEEN'S SCRIBE
(PREVIEW)

Summer 1457
Off the Coast of Cyprus

The merchant galley teetered on a cresting wave and pitched forward with a sickening lurch. Estelle's heart battered her ribs like a leashed falcon desperate to take flight. She drew in a breath, then regretted it. The air in this cramped cabin smelled of sweat and seawater, and her chest felt weighted by stones.

Each time she opened her eyes, there was nothing but blackness, thick and cloying as syrup. Signora Rosso snored lightly beside her, oblivious to Estelle's suffering. Surely, a night had never passed so slowly. When would dawn come? When could she wake her chaperone and escape the galley's hold?

The anxious thoughts came faster and faster, goading her pulse into a wild rhythm. She pressed her hands over her heart, willing it to slow.

Calm yourself. Find the thread of a memory and pull.

She hurtled back in time a dozen years, imagining the oak-studded hills of Auvergne, land of her birth. In her mind's eye, she saw a young girl picking daisies in a lush meadow.

There I am. But where's Étienne?

She conjured up her brother's figure emerging from the shadow of an oak tree, racing through the waist-high grasses.

"Come! The mare's had her foal!"

Estelle smiled in the dark, remembering the joyous exuberance of his shout. She made a circle of her hands, weaving together imaginary daisies. On that long-ago day, had she placed the crown of flowers upon Étienne's head? Kept it for herself? Abandoned it in her excitement to see the newborn foal? Sleepiness crept into her mind like mist, stealthy and silent, ready to claim her.

Then the wavering blare of a horn tore the memory into shreds. She dragged her eyelids open, anticipating the second trumpet blast, the signal that dawn had arrived.

When it came, she said a silent prayer.

A day's voyage left to Cyprus, the captain said last night. Santa Maria, I beg you, protect us on these seas today.

"Signora Rosso," she said. "It's dawn. The trumpeter gave the signal. We can go above decks."

The widow groaned. "Do you ever sleep, child?"

"Not trapped in a ship's cabin, as I've told you each day since we left Rhodes."

Estelle stood, smoothed her wrinkled skirts, straightened her cloak. She longed for a bath.

"Please, signora. You say yourself it's better up there. You can breathe. You can think. The saints hear your prayers—"

"Give me a moment." Signora Rosso's voice was roughened by sleep. "You may be able to spring out of bed light as a feather, girl, but not all of us are seventeen anymore."

Estelle bounced on her toes while the widow hauled herself out of bed, checked the placement of the rosary beads around her neck, and adjusted the folds of her long black cloak.

"I think I've finally got my sea legs. My head's stopped spinning for the first time since we boarded this galley, God be praised." Signora Rosso shuffled to the door and unlatched it. "Carry my cushion, will you?"

"It's already under my arm." Estelle fought an urge to push past her chaperone and take the steps two at a time.

Above decks, the wind had died down to a soft breeze. The ship rolled gently in barely perceptible swells. Crewmen gathered in the bow, receiving orders from their commander for the morning's tasks. The oil lamps lashed to the masts still burned, for fog blurred the horizon in every direction. Soon, though, the sun's rays would warm Estelle's skin, chase away the last tight bands of dread constricting her chest.

She offered her free arm to Signora Rosso. They made their way to the stern, to their usual spot under a waxed canvas shelter. Estelle plopped the cushion on the low box that served as Signora Rosso's seat. Then she sank down on the well-scrubbed oak planks between a neatly coiled flax rope and an unarmed crossbow mounted to the gunwale.

While Signora Rosso closed her eyes and said her prayers, Estelle tipped her head back and took greedy gulps of salt air. A sensation of calm seeped through her body, banishing the agitation she'd been plagued by all night.

The stifling cabin below decks was nothing more than a prison cell. The terror that descended upon her there consumed every fiber of her being—set her heart racing, her limbs trembling, her mind on fire.

"Did you pray to Santa Maria yet?" the widow asked abruptly, her eyes fixed upon Estelle in an accusing stare.

"I was likely the first person aboard to pray to her. Before the crew was up, even."

Signora Rosso snorted. "I doubt that. The holy lady is never far from a sailor's mind."

"Anyone on the sea is at her mercy," Estelle pointed out.

"Especially those who suffer from seasickness, like you and me."

Estelle did not respond. Though she'd never admitted it to Signora Rosso, her problem was not seasickness. But the truth was complicated, and she was a private person.

"What sign were you born under?" Signora Rosso rubbed one of her rosary beads between her forefinger and thumb. It was carved in the shape of a human skull.

"Virgo, with Leo rising."

"Virgos are reasonable people. They tend to be honorable. I don't know you well enough to say for sure, but you're quiet like a Virgo. Leos always seek a battle, yet I see no spark of fire in you." The widow tapped a finger against her lips. "The problem is Virgo's not a water sign, nor is Leo. Once you're off this despicable sea, your health will be restored."

"I hope so," Estelle said.

The widow had not let Estelle out of her sight since they'd left Rhodes last week. Until today, she'd spoken mostly to herself, moaning about her poor health, her hatred of sea voyages, and her husband's relatives in Venice who had never shown kindness until she returned there to oversee the dispensations of his will. This was the first time she'd seemed interested in conversation. But as the morning progressed, Estelle became convinced the woman simply required a pair of ears to absorb her superstitious prattle.

An officer shouted a command in Genoese from the bow deck, and a cabin boy scurried up the mainsail mast. In a moment, his response floated down to the stern.

"They've lost sight of the other ships in our fleet because of the mist," Estelle reported. "They're going to. . ." She cocked her head, straining to hear his message. "Signal the vessels with trumpet blasts and keep the sails lashed until visibility improves," she finished.

The widow gave her an approving nod. "Well done. I still don't understand how a French girl knows Italian so well, especially if you only learned it these past few years."

"My tutor in Rhodes was quite skilled."

The galley shuddered, buffeted by a wave. Estelle grasped the long arm of the crossbow's wooden tiller to steady herself. It shifted under her touch, swinging to point toward the bow deck.

"But you told me a girl taught you." Signora Rosso's eyes narrowed. "Not a tutor."

"I had a girl tutor. Her father is Venetian, and her mother is Greek."

"Telling lies is a grave sin, you know."

Estelle bit back a saucy retort, as she had so many times growing up with a sharp-tongued mother. After a long, steadying breath, it was safe to open her mouth again.

"Girl tutors exist. That's why I'm joining King Jean's court in Cyprus, after all. To be a French tutor."

"So your parents told you." The widow snorted. "But the truth is you're going to Cyprus to find a husband. Why else would a girl your age be sent to a foreign court? Your mother spoke of nothing else when we met."

A flicker of anger ignited in Estelle's belly. She tamped it down, her thoughts straying to those last weeks in Rhodes Town. When the invitation had come for her from King Jean to join the Cypriot court as tutor to his daughter, Princess Charlotte, Maman had been enthusiastic—but she'd never said a word about marriage. Neither had Papa. Both her parents had seen the king's invitation as a great honor. For her part, Estelle had agreed to the plan with both trepidation and excitement. Though she dreaded leaving her family, the thought of being companion to a princess and earning a salary from the royal court of Cyprus made her pride swell.

The trumpets blared a complicated pattern, signaling their location to the rest of the fleet. An answering blast of sounds echoed thinly across the water. Were there three other ships in the fleet? Four? Estelle could not recall.

"Perhaps you'll play at tutoring," Signora Rosso went on, "but in the end you're there to make a match. Is your father a nobleman?"

"Yes, but what does that—"

"King Jean wants French-born nobles in his court," the widow asserted. "That's why you've been summoned. That's your value to the king. You'll see when you get to Nicosia. The capital is full of folk with French names who can't speak their own language."

Wind snaked over the gunwales, carrying a cool tendril of mist that penetrated Estelle's cloak. The lashed sails and riggings thumped and rattled in response to the wind's caress. From the corner of her eye, she saw the ship's cat, an orange tabby with a nicked left ear, trot toward the hold.

"Your best chance of marrying a man who's both noble and rich is in Cyprus, not Rhodes." The widow's voice was softer now, cajoling. "If you marry well, your whole family benefits. You seem intelligent enough. Think it over. In time, you'll agree with me."

Estelle's mind flew to Papa's strange farewell on the dock in Rhodes Town. He'd been oddly nervous in those last moments, tongue-tied, unwilling to meet her gaze. But that had been due to his sorrow at their impending separation, not because he was hiding something from her.

Hadn't it?

Her shoulders stiffened. Could Signora Rosso be right?

"You've got quite a pretty face." The widow leaned closer.

"I imagine you'll have a bevy of suitors. If you're lucky, the king will give you to one of his favorites."

Estelle scrambled to her feet and moved away. The unsettling thought struck her that the woman could be mad. She spouted her strange words with conviction, as if they were carved in stone.

Ignore her. Signora Rosso makes as much sense as a crow jabbering in a tree.

Gripping the gunwale with both hands, Estelle expelled the air in her lungs with a great whoosh. She leaned on her elbows, distracted by a movement in the waves. Then a sudden coldness gripped her chest. Directly below her, a man scrambled up a rope dangling from an iron hook embedded in the ship's hull. Two other figures emerged from the mist, swimming with quiet, powerful strokes toward the galley.

She took a step back, a scream stuck in her throat. In the next instant, the man launched himself over the gunwale.

"God protect us!" Signora Rosso shrieked. "Pirates!"

The man advanced on Estelle, a blade flashing in his hand. In a panic, she grabbed the crossbow's tiller and swung it hard against him. He staggered back, his bare feet tangling in the coiled rope. The dagger clattered to the deck.

"Holy Virgin!" Signora Rosso wailed. "Merciful God! Santa Maria, have pity!"

Estelle snatched up the blade while the man struggled to regain his footing. He steadied himself, then sprang at her.

The terror that had muted her a moment ago was eclipsed by a sudden swell of fury.

"No!"

Thrusting downward with the blade as she shouted the word, she sliced his arm. With a roar of outrage, he lunged for her again.

Footsteps pounded the decks. The air filled with male

voices raised in alarm. Two men pounced on the intruder and pinned him facedown, an arm's length from Signora Rosso. The widow scrabbled her feet away, almost falling off her little box.

Estelle leaped aside as the sailors dragged their captive toward the bow of the ship and other crewmen dispatched his advancing comrades with swords and pikes. The trumpeters issued a series of frantic horn blasts. From afar, other ships in the fleet returned the trumpet calls.

The mist began to lift, revealing a sleek single-masted vessel bobbing nearby. Men swarmed its deck, wielding bows, curved swords, and iron hooks attached to lengths of rope. The dagger trembled in Estelle's clammy palm as a sailor dumped a box of arrows near the crossbow. Had her heart ever pounded this ferociously? She struggled to breathe.

"Pirates!" the sailor bellowed. "Infidels!" He turned to her, snatching the blade from her hand. "Go below, in the name of God!"

Signora Rosso seized Estelle's shoulder. "Move, girl! They'll take us captive otherwise!"

Linking arms with the widow, Estelle pushed through the crush of seamen to the hold. In the cabin, Signora Rosso sank to her knees, babbling a prayer that rose and fell like an endless wave.

Estelle fumbled with the door latch. She pushed her trunk against the door, then flung open the lid. Under her clothes were two items her father had entrusted to her on the dock at Rhodes harbor. One, a book, she cast aside. Then her fingers struck the hard leather of a dagger's sheath.

She drew out the blade.

"What is that?" Signora Rosso asked between sobs, wiping her eyes with the edge of her cloak.

Estelle gripped the polished bone handle. "A gift from my father. I pray I won't have to use it."

When the widow spoke again, her voice was tinged with wonder. "There is fire in you after all, child. I should have known. The stars are never wrong."

HISTORICAL NOTES

This novella, a companion to the Sea and Stone Chronicles collection of novels, features the character Giuliana Rinaldi, a practicing physician trained at the medical school of Salerno. Giuliana is my tribute to a trail-blazing real-life physician, Trotula de Ruggiero (also known as Trota of Salerno and Dame Trot).

The *Schola Medica* of Salerno was believed to be founded around the tenth century and welcomed women during the medieval era. Trotula is the most famous of them, though her story has been nearly lost to time.

Born into a wealthy family in either the eleventh or twelfth century (scholars caution that historical sources from this time period are few and contradictory), Trotula received a high level of education. In addition to practicing medicine, she is believed to have written two treatises on women's health. One of the works pertained to gynecology, the other to cosmetology (providing extensive advice about beauty and health treatments), and both were highly valued as medical treatises by physicians all over Europe throughout the medieval era.

Legend has it that Trotula married a fellow physician and both her sons went on to practice medicine. She was so well-known that stories about her circulated widely in Europe (for example, she's the Dame Trot mentioned in Chaucer's *Canterbury Tales*).

As has been the case for too many women, Trotula vanished from the pages of history over the centuries and doubt was cast upon her very existence. Some scholars maintain that she was a man, skeptical that a woman could have penned texts as important as hers.

The fact remains that Trotula's works informed medicine in medieval Europe for hundreds of years after her death. Among her groundbreaking assertions was the idea that infertility results from *both* female and male reproductive problems (refuting the common belief that women were to blame for inability to conceive). She also advocated using opiates to ease the pain of childbirth, contradicting conventional Christian wisdom.

I am indebted to author Diana Norman (pen name Ariana Franklin). Her wonderful physician character Adelia in the *Mistress of the Art of Death* series introduced me to Salerno's medieval medical school and inspired me to create Giuliana. I'm also grateful for the scholarly research about Trotula available on Academia.edu, particularly the work of Monica H. Green.

For more history about the medieval Mediterranean—including life at sea (where even merchant galleys were armed with mounted swivel guns to repel pirates), knights, falcons, and medical practices—please visit my blog at www.amymaroney.com.

ACKNOWLEDGMENTS

As usual, it took a village to get this story out into the world.

Elizabeth St.John, *merci mille fois* for great writerly advice, ideas, and encouragement every step of the way. Cryssa Bazos, your insights came at the perfect time. Jenny Quinlan, thank you for the excellent editing help. Much appreciation to Rich Farrell and the gang at San Diego Writers, Ink. I'm lucky to have supportive author friends all over the globe, and I'm particularly thankful for the fabulous crew at the Coffee Pot Book Club.

Thank you for the gorgeous cover, Dee Dee Book Covers. Tracey Porter, your map is lovely.

Julie Cassin and Jon Maroney, thank you for reading and appreciating my work in the early stages, and for helping me stay motivated. To my parents, my daughters, and all the family and friends who light up my life—I'm grateful for each one of you.

ABOUT THE AUTHOR

Amy Maroney studied English Literature at Boston University and worked for many years as a writer and editor of nonfiction. She lives in Oregon, U.S.A., with her family. When she's not diving down research rabbit holes, she enjoys hiking, dancing, traveling, and reading. Amy is the author of *The Miramonde Series*, an award-winning art mystery trilogy about a Renaissance-era female artist and the modern-day scholar on her trail. Her romantic suspense novels, the *Sea and Stone Chronicles*, are set in 15th-century Rhodes and Cyprus.

Join Amy's community of readers and get monthly updates about her research and next books (plus great deals on historical fiction) at www.amymaroney.com.

If you enjoyed this book, please take a moment to leave a review online or spread the word to family and friends.

facebook.com/amymaroneyauthor

x.com/wilaroney

instagram.com/amymaroneywrites

bookbub.com/authors/amy-maroney

amazon.com/stores/Amy-Maroney/author/B01LYHPXEO

pinterest.com/amyloveshistory